# Revolving Door

Veronica Bower-Feek

First published in Great Britain by Lulu in 2013

ISBN: 978-1-291-33322-0

Book Jacket by Catherine Palmer

## FOREWORD

The characters in this book are fictional, but the problems faced by many prisoners on their release from prison, are not.

In writing this book I draw from my own experiences working within the criminal justice system for the last twelve years.

Of all of earth's creatures, only Man does not have the *right* to build a home.

It is therefore incumbent on civilised society to ensure that appropriate shelter is provided.

The problems faced by 'revolving door' prisoners are often complex and entrenched.

Some have drug and alcohol issues, and many suffer from poor mental health.

There are several agencies concerned with the rehabilitation of offenders, not least The Probation Service, but their efforts are frequently undermined by the homeless status of their clients.

If the primary needs of shelter and food are not met, these men and women, are destined to re-offend.

Until we as a society take seriously these basic rights, the revolving door will continue.

*This book is dedicated to my children through whom I have learnt so much.*
*They are Mark, Gemma, Charley and Jonathan.*
*To Adrian Pearson, for all his unending support, I pledge my love and loyalty.*
*Finally, I would like to acknowledge The Probation Service who strive so hard in the rehabilitation of offenders but are themselves under threat of dismantlement.*

# REVOLVING DOOR

It was 8:30 am and I'd finished being processed. I'd changed into my clothes, collected my discharge grant and was about to be thrown back into the world.

Nervously, I waited with the Screw whilst he radioed for permission to take me to the gate. You were never *free* until you were OUT. I knew that from experience.

The old gate was unlocked and I stepped over the frame into a British winter. *FREE*! I thought, for a moment euphoric, but my high was quickly replaced by a sense of impending failure. I had been here before.

They'd given me directions to the station after I'd had the 'don't do it again and hope we don't see you again' chat, but I didn't need them. This was my home, or at least what served as home, and I knew my way to the Council and the Job Centre. Not that I'd be getting a job any time soon, I thought. But I'd need a crisis loan to see me through the next few days and I could use the phone from there.

The noise of the outside world was strange even though I'd only been inside for a few months, and for a minute I just stood there taking it in. But then the day shift started to arrive and I needed to go. These were the faces that I wanted to forget.

As I walked down the hill to the town I wondered where I should go first. It was tempting to go to the pub to celebrate my release, but I'd promised myself that this time it would be different. This time I'd do it right.

*I'm free*, I thought, I can do what I bloody like! But this wasn't true, and I knew it. All I had was my discharge grant and the clothes I stood up in. I'd gone to prison homeless and come out the same way. At least I still have my phone, I thought, but where the fuck was the charger? I'd have to try to remember where I'd stayed the night before I was arrested. Hopefully it might have been at a mate's house rather than on the streets. What mates? I thought, amused at my attempt at self deception. And I knew that my charger was gone.

For a moment I felt a bit unsteady, the traffic noise and my thoughts causing my head to spin. I needed a drink. Just *one* whilst I came up with a plan. Somehow, the previous night's plan, which had seemed so simple in the comfort of my cell, no longer seemed possible.

The pub was warm and friendly and for the first time since I stepped out of the gate I felt safe. This was home. This I knew.

I sat down near the window and just watched, waiting for something to happen, waiting for a plan.

By lunchtime I was on my fourth pint and the world seemed pretty friendly, a plan unnecessary. I must find somewhere to crash, though, I thought. So I got up, unsteadily, and headed for the door.

'Hey Mick… Is that you?' asked a voice from somewhere behind me. I spun round to see one of my mates.
'Alright Dave?' I replied, 'I just got out. What's been happening? Want a drink?'
And I found myself at the bar again holding out the last of my £20 notes.

Dave wasn't a great mate, and I didn't really care what he'd been doing whilst I'd been away, but I needed a place to sleep and he'd do as well as anyone else, so I chatted to him affably and listened to all his shit.

'And that's what I told Marcia,' he said, 'and she fucking blew me out! And now I'm out on my ear and staying with Phil.'

Oh well, I thought, that's that plan out the window and it cost me three quid. Fuck, fuck, fuck!
'I've got to go Dave,' I said as soon as I could get a word in. 'Got to sign on and all that shit. Hope it works out with Marcia!'
And I got up for the second time, this time making it through the door.

******

It hadn't always been like this. Somewhere, in another lifetime, things had been pretty normal. Family, normal, school normal. Me, my mum, my dad and my sister. *NORMAL*

Like the time me and my sister, Sammy, had sat on top of a slate heap, our legs swinging in free space, eating honey sandwiches. *That*, I'd never forget.

It was a clear summer's day in July and we'd travelled up the night before in Dad's old Morris, the car straining under the weight of our cases and supplies. It had taken forever to get there, 6 hours I think, but I remember not minding the journey because there was so much to look at as we sped through different counties gradually climbing into the mountains of Wales.
It was late by the time we arrived and getting dark, but the lights were on in the cottage we'd rented and as we drove up the path it seemed to beckon us with a friendly smile.

Sammy was two years younger than me and we were both really excited. She had lovely long blonde hair, I remember, and when we got up to explore the next morning I noticed that it nearly touched the tops of her Wellington boots.

'Come on Sammy,' I said 'Let's go out and look for treasure. There must be loads in these mountains cos there's mines here, Dad says.'
'What sort of mines?' replied Sammy 'Will there be diamonds?
I laughed and grabbed her hand. 'No, silly. Everyone knows there aren't any diamond mines in England, and anyway, Dad said they're slate.'
'What's slate?' she said her eyes shining with excitement. But I didn't know so I changed the subject quickly as we ran out into the sunshine.

8

The cottage was perched on the side of a hill and the path we'd driven up the night before seemed to carry on so Sammy and I headed upwards. At first it was stony and difficult to walk on, but after about ten minutes it turned into grass and Sammy and I sat down and took off our shoes, revelling in the feel of the grass between our toes.

'I'm hungry,' she said looking wistfully at our packet of sandwiches. 'What's in them , Mickey? Can we have one now?'

But I didn't want to stop yet as the adventure had barely begun. 'It's too early and Mum said the sandwiches are a surprise.' I said sternly. 'You'll have to wait.'

'S'not fair,' she grumbled before turning her attention to a daisy which had wedged between her toes. 'I want a sandwich!'

******

'Watch out Idiot!' shouted a voice from somewhere to my right, an arm grabbing mine. 'You were nearly mincemeat!'

My reverie broke, the sun replaced by gray pavement. 'Bloody Hell!' I exclaimed. I haven't seen you for years John! I must have been daydreaming.'

'Drunk, more like,' he said, punching me on the arm. 'Same old Mick then... What've you been up to?'

9

'Not much,' I replied, unsure how much he knew. But he looked at me sideways and I knew I didn't have to pretend.

'I just got out today,' I explained 'and I'm finding my feet. Well the pub actually,' I laughed, but I need somewhere to stay tonight so I thought I'd better see who's in The Lamb.'

'Haven't you heard?' exclaimed John. The Lamb burnt down a couple of months ago. I thought *you lot* watched telly inside. It was all over the news.

'Shit! What happened? Was anyone hurt?' I exclaimed. 'And where does everyone go now? I can't believe it's not there any more.'

'It wasn't arson,' he replied, 'though everyone thought it was at the time. Seems like a dippy barmaid left some candles burning when she closed up and you know how draughty that place was. Caught the curtains and that was that. One hell of a blaze by the way. We were up most of the night watching it.'

I took this in at first with amazement and then with concern. The lamb was my main haunt and everyone went there. Somewhere in my mind it was part of my plan. *Shit!*

'So where does everyone go now?' I asked again urgently. But John was looking at his watch and had lost interest. 'Don't know Mick. Sorry. They weren't really my crowd. It was just my local. Got to go now mate. Sorry. I'll see you around.' And he was gone, striding purposefully up the hill.

It was beginning to get dark now, and I was shivering with cold. Fuck, what now? I thought. So

I sat down on a damp looking bench to roll a fag and think.


\*\*\*\*\*\*


The sandwiches were honey and Sammy and I sat on the *slate mountain* devouring them hungrily.

'What shall we do now? she asked me excitedly, her bright blue eyes shining in the sun. 'Can we look for treasure?'
But I wasn't paying attention because I was studying a worm that was crawling too close to the edge of the pit, so it was only when she grabbed my arm and pinched me that I came to.
'What?' I growled, sounding more annoyed than I actually was. 'Let's just sit here for a while, can't we? I like it here and anyway we'd better not go too far in case Mum worries.'
'What's that?' Sammy exclaimed a second later, pointing up to the sky. 'It looks like it's swooping down to get us!
'An eagle, I think' I said uncertainly. 'You read too many fairy stories Sammy. It's not big enough to lift us.' But I wasn't sure, and suddenly we didn't seem so safe, so I jumped up and shouted to Sammy to follow me, laughing more bravely than I felt as we ran down the hill and away from the monster in the sky.

When we got back to the cottage we were puffed out and we burst through the door babbling our story incomprehensibly.

'And there was this great monster bird in the sky!' exclaimed Sammy 'And Mickey said I was being silly but then he ran away.'

'Well, well,' said our Dad trying to sound interested. 'Sounds like you two are having fun. Why don't you go out and see what else you can find. When I was your age I was out all day.'

'Can we eat the sandwiches?' Sammy asked as she grabbed my hand and pulled me towards the door again.'

'Of course,' he nodded, returning to his paper and sighing contentedly. 'That's what they're for!'

That was a great holiday, I mused, suddenly back on the bench with a half finished roll up dangling from my fingers. But it was a lifetime ago and right now I was in trouble.... Perhaps if I toured the pubs I would find someone I knew, I thought. But I'd already spent half of my discharge grant so I got up and wandered down the High Street instead. It was looking like a night on the streets, I realised, and my best option was to find somewhere out of the wind.

## DAY TWO

I spent that night, uncomfortable and cold, in the
shelter of a shop doorway. It hadn't rained, thank
God, but I was stiff with cold when I stood up and
my limbs didn't seem to work. 'You've become
soft,' I said to myself sharply. 'Come on, Mickey.
You're free.' And I looked up at the sky willing it to
get light.

When dawn arrived it was grey and unpromising,
the shriek of gulls filling the air and a damp mist
hanging around the street lamps.
For a moment I wished I was back in my cell eating
my breakfast and watching telly. But I didn't really
want that, I just wanted things to be better. Let's go
Mickey! I geed myself up as I headed to the nearest
bakery to wait for it to open. It's breakfast time.

By nine o'clock I was full and warm and on my
way to The Job Centre to start a new claim. The sky
was still grey, a cool wind blowing, but somewhere
there was a hint of brightness and even a streak of
blue, so perhaps it would warm up later.

The first person I recognised at the Job Centre was
the rather large and somewhat scruffy, security
guard 'Hello mate, still here, then,' I chirped,
giving him a friendly punch on the arm. 'I'm back
again!'

The Job Centre was the same as always, the
atmosphere unchanging over time, but today there

were unfamiliar faces behind the desks. Bugger, I thought. It was much easier when I didn't have to explain the whole story. Thank goodness it was early so I wouldn't have to wait too long. The place depressed me.

By ten thirty I'd made my claim with 'Sarah', who looked about twelve and spoke like she was in an episode of Friends. I had hoped to get a crisis loan, but I was told it would take a couple of days before my claim was on the system and until then I was entitled to nothing. I *have* to find someone to stay with, I thought as I left. I'm not up to another cold night.

It was still too early to trawl the pubs looking for my mates so I decided to go straight to the housing department and present myself as homeless. I'd done this many times before and I knew what they'd say, but sometimes you got lucky and they shipped you off to a B&B whilst they assessed you. I didn't think it was likely, this time though, but I had nothing better to do and at least it would be warm.

As soon as I walked into the housing office I knew that I'd be walking out with nothing. It was my *favourite* housing officer behind the screen and I saw her hackles rise.
'Back again so soon,' she snapped with no attempt to hide her contempt as she got out the dreaded form from under her desk. 'What can I do for you?'

The previous year I'd made the mistake of making myself *intentionally* homeless by being late with my rent. This *officer* had given me the good news that the council had no obligation to help me. The fact that my Housing Benefit payment had got screwed up because I started to work part time and it took them weeks to reassess, was apparently beside the point. I had clearly *wanted* to be back on the streets so it was intentional!

'I'm homeless again,' I said, through gritted teeth. 'and I've just been released from Prison so I thought I might be priority need...... But I didn't even listen to her reply, her tone was enough, and after a few minutes I got up and left.


Outside it had finally brightened and suddenly the world seemed a little less hostile.

The town, which was beginning to buzz with morning shoppers, was coming alive and with nothing else to do, I sat down on a bench overlooking the river and rolled a fag, for a moment enjoying the sense of freedom so recently denied me. The river was flowing fast, the high tide approaching, and I watched with interest as a boat perched on a concrete shelf gradually righted itself, its mast moving as if by magic till it stood proud and straight.

In the distance I could see a pair of swans trying to swim against the flow, their large webbed feet paddling like crazy, but they soon gave up, the effort apparently not worth it, and I laughed as they were swept down river, their feathers ruffling in the wind.

Their life was so simple, I thought, sadly. Why was mine so hard? And my thoughts started to tumble over each other in desperation to find a solution before the darkness set in again.

'One thing at a time, mate' I told myself sternly, stubbing my fag on top of the bin. Perhaps there would be one of my mates hanging around outside Probation.

As I walked towards the building that housed The Court and Probation my spirits lifted a little. There was almost as much chance that I'd bump into someone I knew there as in *The Lamb*. 'Hello,' I waved at the security guard on the door. 'Anything interesting happening?'

But she was busy searching people with her magnetic wand so she didn't reply. I wasn't offended though. I knew her well and she was just busy.

'How're you doing Mickey?' said a voice from behind me. I turned round expectantly, ready with my story, but it was a Probation Officer I'd had before and although she was good there'd be nothing she could do.

'OK Miss.' I said. The prison habit dying hard. 'I've just got out.'

'Are you reporting on licence?' she asked 'I don't remember seeing your name on the new allocations.

'Not this time,' I smiled. 'I didn't get long enough.

'What a shame,' she replied knowingly. 'I hope you've got somewhere to live?'

But she was clearly in a hurry, and was already disappearing up the stairs, so I just shook my head.

16

By now there was a babble of conversation coming from upstairs and I thought I heard one or two familiar voices but I wasn't sure. Perhaps they would come down for a fag, I thought.

'How's it going?' I said to the security guard who had finished searching and was looking bored. 'Any gossip? I've just got out...'
'I thought we hadn't seen you for a while,' she smiled. 'How long did you do this time?'
'Not long enough,' I replied. 'So I'm not on licence and can't even get help from Probation. Not that there'd be much they could do with the housing,' I qualified. 'But at least I'd have had someone to talk to other than myself.'
'Know what you mean,' she said. 'I hear that a lot.'
'You don't know of any rooms going do you?' I asked, hopefully.
But she shook her head, and someone was coming in, so I disappeared outside.

For a while I just hung around and smoked, watching the passers by as they hurried about their business, waiting for something. Waiting for opening time.

'Got a spare fag mate?' said a voice from the doorway. 'I've only got a couple of minutes.'
'Sure.' I replied handing him the tobacco. But he handed it back to me with shaking hands.
'Could I twos yours? he asked. 'I just need a puff.'
'Due up?' I asked, handing him the roll-up. 'How's it looking?'

17

'Not good,' he shook his head. 'But you never know do you. I was sure I was going down last time and they gave me Probation. What you here for?'

'Just waiting for a friend this time.' I smiled. 'Good luck.'

And he handed me back the bedraggled fag which I stubbed out as soon as he'd gone.

*This....,*I thought, is my life...


\*\*\*\*\*\*


After Wales, life went on as it had before and the next thing to happen was Xmas. Sammy and I loved Xmas, it was always so exciting. But this year I had asked for something special and I couldn't wait.

The school term seemed to drag on for ever, each day lasting a hundred years, but finally the last day arrived and the holidays were starting.

Sammy and I ran to school, that day, each of us clutching a bag of cakes that mum had made for the party. 'Hurry up!' I remember shouting as I looked up to the sky searching for snow. 'It's almost Christmas!'


By Christmas Eve I was too excited to sleep, the anticipation of Father Christmas too much to bear, but sometime later I must have drifted off because suddenly it was light and Sammy was jumping on me.

'Wake up Mickey!' she shouted in my ear. 'I've already opened mine! Come on, lazy coach!'

She hoiked my bulging stocking up onto the bed. 'It's Christmas Day!'

The stocking contained the usual array of toys, games and Satsumas, and I pulled each one out happily, accompanied by squeals of delight from Sammy who had by now dragged in her haul as well.
'We've got the same amount,' she announced as if all was right in the world. 'But mine are more girly and they're better.'

Christmas always followed the same pattern in our family, the main presents being opened after breakfast, but Sammy and I ran downstairs anyway, hoping to speed things up.
'You'll have to wait,' laughed mum. 'Dad's still getting dressed and we're having breakfast together. Why don't you lay the table and surprise him?'
Normally, this suggestion would have produced a round of moans from Sammy and me, but today we went off willingly, the spreads and cereals balanced precariously on a tray.

After breakfast, which seemed to last forever, Mum made us help clear up.
'Is it time now?' asked Sammy, her eyes shining with excitement. 'Can we open our presents?'
But Mum and Dad always made us do them one at a time with everyone watching and Dad was on guard by the Christmas tree so we couldn't even peek.

'Right,' he said. 'I'm going to be *Father Christmas* so who shall we have first?'

*'**ME!**'* we both shouted at the tops of our voices, the excitement almost palpable, *'**ME**...'*

The present opening took some time and normally I didn't mind as I enjoyed seeing everyone else's pleasure, but as the pile got smaller and I could see round the tree, I was getting worried.
'Are there any more?' I blurted, unable to stop myself. 'Where's my main one?'
'Hmmm. Let me see,' replied Dad thoughtfully. 'No I think that's the lot. Can you see any more, Sammy?'
My face crashed, hot tears starting to form in my lumpy throat.'
'Only joking!' Dad exclaimed. 'Shut your eyes and count to thirty.'

******

'Got another fag mate?' said a voice I vaguely recognised. But it was the bloke from earlier who had obviously escaped custody, and I must have looked disappointed because he said, 'What's up? You look like you've swallowed a tenner. Don't worry about the fag, mate, I was only asking.'
'No. You're alright mate.' I apologised, handing him the tobacco. 'I was remembering stuff that's all. How'd it go?'
'Community Order.' He replied looking relieved. 'I was bloody lucky cos it was a soft bench.'
'Not the DJ then,' I laughed. 'Well that sounds like a reason to celebrate. Fancy a drink?'

20

'Sure,' he replied. 'The Crown's cheap. Let's go there.'

By the time we'd got to the third pint we were friends; our shared experiences of Court and Prison, bonding us quickly.
'I need a place to crash for a few nights mate,' I stated. 'Any chance?'
'Sure,' he said. 'It will be good to have some company for a change. 'You get the floor though, or you can sleep in an armchair if you like.'
'Anything,' I replied with relief. 'I owe you big time, mate. Thanks.'
'You haven't seen the gaff yet,' he laughed. 'You might prefer the streets!'
'Yeah, right,' I replied sarcastically. 'I love freezing my nuts off in a shop doorway!'

My new friend's name was Daryl but his friends called him Das.
Das was 28, a bit older than me, and Das had been a naughty boy, but Das was my friend now, the best one I had, and for the next few hours I indulged him by listening to his *war stories*.
'And that's when I thought, Das my boy, it's time to grow up,' he smiled. 'but I just needed a little dosh to set me up. Just one more job.....'

Fancy a spliff?' he asked as he got his grinder out from under the sofa.
'Yes.. No.. well I'm trying not to.. but fuck that,' I said, seeing his disappointment. 'It's only a spliff. I'll be OK so long as I stay off the smack.'

'That's what I reckon,' he agreed seriously 'and so far I'm sticking to it. Let's get wrecked!

\*\*\*\*\*\*

My *present* ran into the sitting room wagging his tail and barking. Mum had tied a ribbon round his neck which he was trying to remove and in his excitement he caught his foot in it and fell over.

'Meet Fudge,' laughed Dad. 'You're going to have your hands full, son, but I must admit he's lovely.'
'He's fantastic!' I exclaimed. 'Thank you Mum. Thank you Dad. I'll look after him really well, I promise you.'
And I rolled on the floor with my new puppy, happier than I could ever remember feeling.

## DAY THREE

It was warm in the flat and I slept well despite the
hard floor. Das was still asleep when I woke up, but
it was light so I figured it couldn't be too early.
I sat down in one of the arm chairs with a cup of tea
and a fag, and for the first time since my release I
felt a glimmer of hope. If I could stay till I found
somewhere else I might stand half a chance, I
thought. I just needed a chance.

I looked around me at the debris from last night's
session and realised that at sometime we must have
ordered a pizza. Shit! I hope I didn't pay for it, I
thought, alarm coursing through my veins. But my
money was still buried in my bag so it must have
been Das, thank fuck. Looks like cold pizza for
breakfast then, I thought, but I decided to wait and
ask him.

The room was small and snug with two shabby
armchairs and a drop leaf table in front of them. I'd
had to move the table to make room to lie down so
now I moved it back; the dents in the carpet making
it easy to see where it had been.
Once I'd moved the table I could see the TV so I
switched it on, keen for the familiarity of my old
routine.
Despite being close to the town the flat was quiet,
and for a moment I missed the hub bub of jail. Shit,
I thought I'm in danger of becoming
institutionalised, and once that happened you were
lost.

For a while I sat in the chair wondering what to do next, but however hard I tried I couldn't think of anything beyond getting my crisis loan so I lit another fag. I'd been told 3 days by 'Sarah', but sometimes they were quicker so it was probably worth going to the job centre to ask, if only for the exercise.

'Fucking Hell, mate! It's the middle of the bloody night. Why you up so early?' Exclaimed a grumpy voice from kitchen. 'I haven't seen this time of day for months!'
'Sorry Mate,' I apologised. 'force of habit I guess. What time is it?'
'About 8 I think.'
Das sounded pissed off. 'I'm going back to bed.'
'Will you be in later if I go out for a bit?' I asked. But he'd shut his door and didn't reply so I'd just have to chance it.

Das was wrong about the time, it was close to 9 according to the clock by the memorial. Good. I thought, the bakery will be open. Eating Das's pizza didn't seem such a good idea after waking him up. We were *friends* last night after 3 pints and a few spliffs, but in the cold light of day ………'

I could smell the bakery long before I saw it and by the time I got there I was almost salivating. 'I'll have a steak pie and a coffee luv,' I said to the girl behind the counter. 'Can you make sure it's nice and hot?'

24

'They're all hot,' she sounded bored. 'And so's the coffee. That'll be £1.80.'
'Thanks,' I said, determined not to let her ruin my mood. 'Have a lovely day.'

The weather was bright and warmer so I sat on a bench by the river, eating my pie contentedly. I'd left a note for Das so he knew I was coming back, but I reckoned it'd be best if I stayed out for a while so he could have some space. The last thing I wanted was to piss him off again, and anyway, the job centre would be open now.

Inside the job centre I got that familiar feeling of time standing still, but this time there was a familiar face.
'Morning Sally,' I chirped. 'How are you doing?'
'Better than you, I reckon,' she replied looking at my dishevelled clothes. 'are you sleeping rough again, Mickey?'
'Sort of,' I smiled. 'you know what it's like. I just want to know if my claim's active yet. Can you check?
'Sure,' she replied. 'take a seat. My computer's still warming up so we could be here for a while!'

Half an hour later I walked out of the job centre jubilantly. My claim was active and the signs were good for a crisis loan. I'd made the application over the phone and the interviewer seemed confident that I'd get it, so all I had to do now was to wait for a call. I'd been worried about that part as my phone's battery was still flat, but Sally had agreed that they could ring me on her phone at 2 pm so that was sorted too.

The weather was even better now, the sun shining out of a clear blue sky, so I decided to get a can of Fosters and walk along the river.

\*\*\*\*\*\*

The river was sparkling in the sun, a slight ripple the only evidence of the breeze. 'Come on Sammy,' I urged. 'We're late and Mum will kill us if it gets dark.'

'I'm tired,' she replied grumpily. 'Can't we sit down for a while? My feet are hurting.'

'No.' I said firmly. 'We promised we'd be back by 6 and it's nearly that now. Let's pretend we've escaped from a nasty witch and we're running for our lives!'

'Is there really witches?' she said, somewhat missing the point of my challenge. 'Dad says you make stuff up, and anyway I don't believe in them so I'm not scared.' She sat down huffily taking off her sandals.

'Why are you taking your shoes off? I barked. 'I'm serious Sammy, we have to get going!'

'Got stones in them,' she spat back. 'Do you *want* me to hurt myself?'

'Of course not,' I softened, concerned that her stubborn streak would delay us further. 'Let me see….'

This time we were in Cornwall, again staying in a little cottage. It was late August, the night's already drawing in, but it was still hot and life was an adventure.

The day before we'd gone for a walk with Mum, Dad and Fudge; the path meandering for miles along the coast, ending up at a tiny cove.

Fudge was in his seventh heaven, the smells of the woods and sea acting like a propellant. 'Here Fudge,' I called, waving an imaginary stick. 'what's this?' But he wasn't falling for my trickery and only stopped for the briefest of moments.

'It's not fair, Dad,' I moaned. 'I want to play with him and he just wants to run.'

'He's a dog, Mickey,' he laughed. 'Let's play a trick on Mum!

'What trick?' I whispered excitedly as Dad stopped and pretended to tie his boot lace.

'I'm going to fall over,' he whispered back, 'and pretend I've broken my ankle. That should get the girls going!'

'OK' I said, trying to sound excited. But I wasn't sure that Mum would find it funny, and Sammy would probably cry.

'Ow. Ow!' he cried, loudly as he fell dramatically to the ground. 'Help, Mickey, I think I've hurt myself.'

'They're coming!' I exclaimed in a whisper. 'And so is Fudge!'

Fudge arrived at break neck speed screeching to a halt like Scooby Doo. 'It's alright, Fudge,' I reassured. He's just pretending.'

But fudge didn't *get* our game and he was licking
Dad's face as if his life depended on it.
'Stop it, Fudge!' he urged in a loud whisper. 'I'm
fine.'
And for a moment he stopped, his head cocked on
one side with a quizzical look on his face.
'Ow...' cried Dad to the approaching girls. 'I think
I've broken my ankle.'
But this was too much for Fudge and he leapt up
and started to drag Dad by his coat, the collar
making an ominous ripping sound.

Mum and Sammy were careering down the path, by
now,  sticks scattering in their wake, their faces
etched with concern. And I turned away so they
couldn't see my face, desperately trying to stifle my
laughter. But now the scene was so funny that I
couldn't help myself and I burst into hysterical fits,
further confusing Fudge who was spitting out bits of
collar.


******


'Oy! Watch my line!' shouted a grumpy looking
fisherman. 'You blind or something?
And Cornwall became Sussex.

I enjoyed my walk along the river despite my
reverie being broken, but now it was time to go
back to the job centre. The sky had clouded over
whilst I was walking, everything turning grey, but
the promise of money in my pocket was keeping me

28

cheerful and I found myself whistling. Things could be worse, Mickey, I told myself. Things are on the up.

The job centre was busy, the waiting area full of late sleepers, but I was waved through by security who had spotted Sally beckoning to me.
'Good timing,' she said, holding out the phone. 'It's for you.'

By 3 o'clock I was walking out with a Giro and heading uphill to the Post Office.

'You'll need ID with that,' said the fat red faced woman behind the counter, feigning politeness. But I was prepared for this and I passed over a letter from the job centre confirming my identity.
'It needs to be photo ID,' she said, sounding pleased. 'We close at 5.30.'
'I've just come out of prison and I don't have any.' I told her patiently, used to this merry-go-round. 'Can you check with your Manager, please, I've done this before and the letter's always been accepted.'
But she wasn't going to budge and the queue was getting restless so rather than create a scene I left.
'Fuck.' What now....
Outside the Post Office I rolled a fag. Why was everything so fucking difficult?
Half an hour later I tried again, this time juggling my position to make sure I was seen by someone less hostile.
'How do you want the money?' She was bored and had scarcely looked at my letter.

29

'As it comes,' I replied with relief, holding out my hand for the *eighty three pounds and forty six pence*. 'Thank you.'

By the time I left the Post Office the day and the light were both fading. Half past four, I murmured, checking the clock. I'll just have a quick pint before going home.

By the time I got back, Das was well and truly up, loud music evident before I even got to the door. 'Hello mate,' he said as he answered the door. 'Thought you might have been arrested again! I've got a few friends round.'

The room was full of smoke, several large spliffs doing the rounds, and I sat down nervously. This was too crowded for my liking. 'Alright?' I said to room in general, but all I got were a few nods and I realised that they were too stoned to care.
'What you been up to?' asked Das. 'Get any money?'
'I'll tell you later,' I replied cautiously. 'would it be alright if I have a shower? I'm whacked!'
'Sure,' he replied. 'Help yourself. The towel on the rad's only been used a couple of times.' He sat down again in time to take control of a spliff. '

By the time I got out of the shower most of Das's friends were leaving.
'We're going to watch the game at the White Horse,' he explained. 'You can come if you've got some dosh.'

'Think I'll give it a miss, but thanks anyway,' I replied. 'Takes me a few days if you know what I mean.'
'OK. See you later. When you need to crash just move the table again.'
He opened the door, his friends and the smoke billowing out together.

Alone in the flat I felt a sense of peace. This was what I wanted and it felt good. But Das wouldn't put up with me for long, I was sure of that, and the thought kept nagging at me.
I switched on the TV, just in time to catch the end of The Simpsons, and stretched out on the floor, luxuriating in the warmth and space.

The next thing I knew it was 10 o'clock and the TV was blaring incomprehensibly. I switched over to BBC 1, the news preferable to whatever it was that woke me up.

\*\*\*\*\*\*

'Get up Dad!' commanded Sammy. I know you're messing about because Mickey's laughing....'
'It's cruel to laugh when someone's hurt themselves,' retorted Dad, trying to keep up the pretence. But a smile was cracking his face and we all fell about except Mum.
'It's not Funny, John,' she chided. 'I could have broken *my* ankle, running to rescue you.'

But there was a hint of a smile on her face too and soon we all dropped to the ground in a heap, laughing uncontrollably.
'Woof!' barked Fudge uncertainly as he jumped into the melee, all legs and claws, 'WOOF...'

By the time we got back to the village it was dark, a ring of fairy lights casting playful shadows around the small grey walled harbour.
The cottage was in a tiny cobbled street, its door opening onto the road, and after the long walk it was a welcome sight so we went in sighing with pleasure.
'Come and help me light the fire, Mickey,' said Dad. 'I think Mum's going to run a bath for Sammy.
'Can't I help with the fire?' moaned Sammy, trying to pull away from Mum's hand. But Mum's grip was firm and two seconds later Sammy's ponytail disappeared up the narrow stair case.

Dad was an expert at lighting fires, usually telling me about his days in the scouts whilst he was doing so, but this time he had something else in mind.
'You can do it if you like,' he suggested. 'you've seen me do it often enough.'
'Can I really!' I exclaimed, a warm glow of pride sweeping over me. Fire lighting was a *Man* thing, and Dad was letting me do it!

There was no fire at Das's and I was getting cold.
Time for bed I thought, dragging the blanket from
behind the arm chair. I'm knackered.

# DAY FOUR

When I woke in the morning I could vaguely
remember being tripped over in the middle of the
night. Outside it was windy, the rain lashing against
the window, but despite being on the floor I was
warm and comfortable. I wanted a cup of tea and
was dying for a fag, but this time I wouldn't wake
Das up. Cautiously I opened the kitchen door,
listening for any movement, but all was quiet from
his room and I figured I could get away with boiling
the kettle.
I need my own place. I thought ruefully. I just need
a room.
By the time I'd had my first tea I'd stopped feeling
sorry for myself.
Right. I thought, picking up the end of a spliff from
an ashtray. What now?

At eleven o'clock Das was still asleep so I scribbled
him a note and crept out. He'd left me a key, which
was amazing considering how late he'd got in, and I
put it into my pocket gratefully.

The rain had eased off a bit, the wind not so vicious,
but it was far from a nice day and I turned up my
jacket collar as I walked down the hill.
I'd spent the morning thinking and smoking, trying
to work out my next move, but all I'd come up with
was what I usually did so I headed towards the train
station.
'Return to Eastbourne, please,' I reqested handing
over a fiver. A ticket spewed out of the machine as

34

if by magic, the clerk hardly acknowledging me.
'Which platform is it?' I asked to annoy him, but I
was elbowed out the way by a teenager with a
buggy so I didn't hear the reply.

On platform two there was a café, so as I hadn't
eaten, I headed there first.
'Can I have a bacon sandwich please?' I asked
cheerfully, so happy to have some money in my
pocket. 'And a cup of tea.'

By the time I got to Eastbourne I knew I'd be facing
a long queue at the busy Housing Advice Centre. I'd
rolled a few fags for the wait and bought a quarter
bottle of vodka to keep the cold out, but amazingly
there wasn't a queue. Must be the weather. I thought
cheerfully.
There were two people in front of me and just for a
change there were two staff on duty.
'How can I help?' His name was Tim according to
his badge. 'Take a seat.'

Tim was a good listener and fifteen minutes later he
seemed to have a handle on my story.
'The thing is,' he explained 'you should have
appealed when they said you were intentionally
homeless because you didn't contribute to it
happening.'
'That's what I thought at the time,' I replied. 'But
they said I'd be wasting my time.'
'They always do that,' he sighed. 'It's part of their
strategy, but you'd probably have won. There's not
much we can do retrospectively but I think we can
argue for a reassessment.'

'How long will it take?' I asked, slightly surprised that there was *anything* we could do. 'I don't think I'll be able to stay where I am very long.'

'Anything up to a month, I'm afraid and whatever you do don't tell them you've got somewhere to stay. I know it's only temporary, but they won't see it like that.'

'I know.' I replied. I've been bitten by that one before.

'OK, well I'll start the process and get in touch as soon as anything develops. What's your number?'

I gave Tim my phone number, explaining that it might be a couple of days before it was working, and left feeling almost hopeful. If I could just get somewhere to live I knew I could make it. This time I could make it.

It was late afternoon by the time I got back and I decided to go straight to the flat. I was tempted to call into the pub for a well deserved beer, but for once I managed to overrule myself, instead getting a sandwich from the supermarket.

When I got *home* I let myself in quietly and headed for the kitchen. 'You in Das?' I asked. But there was no response so I guessed he was out.

Good, I thought, I can have a bit of time on my own again....

By 9pm there was till no sign of Das and I decided to have a shower. I undressed hurriedly, dropping my clothes on the floor, but then I saw that the

36

towel had gone. Shit! I'd have to look for another one.
I checked a couple of cupboards and glanced around the living room but I couldn't see one anywhere. Must be in the bedroom, I thought, cautiously opening the door.

It was dark in the bedroom, the curtains still closed, and for a moment all I could see were shadows. 'Sorry mate.' I whispered to the lump in the bed. But he didn't reply or even stir. 'You alright mate?' I asked in a louder whisper. 'I just need a towel.... **DAS!** I shouted to the still form in the bed, 'Wake up, mate you're scaring me!' But Das didn't wake up and now I started to shake.

For a few moments I just stood there in disbelief Fucking Hell, he's not bloody moving, I thought. I don't fucking believe it!
I turned on the light, hoping I was imagining things, but the light just made matters worse. Das was lying on his back, his eyes wide and staring. Das was definitely *dead.*


By the time the police had gone and Das had been carted off it was 4 am. I'd given my statement, limited though it was, and for the moment at least it looked like I was off the hook. Fortunately for me they'd found an empty needle in the bed and Das was a known user.

The flat had taken on a surreal appearance, the place feeling ghostly now, but I knew it was probably shock and tiredness so I stretched out on the floor. I s'pose I could sleep on the bed, I thought fleetingly. But I knew I couldn't.

******

The morning after I'd made my first fire it was raining. 'What can we do Mickey?' whined Sammy. 'I want to go hunting for gold.'
'You don't *hunt for gold.'* I retorted 'You mine it. And anyway it's not real gold, it's fools gold.'
'Does that mean it's *silly*?' asked Sammy in a baby voice. But I didn't reply because something had caught my attention.
'Can you hear that?' I exclaimed, running to the door. 'It sounds like a helicopter!'
'Where?' asked Sammy looking round the room. 'I can't hear anything.'
'That's 'cos you're deaf.' I said grabbing her arm. 'Come on. Let's go and look.'
Sammy and I ran down the narrow cobbled street following the sound of the whirring blades.
'Look Mickey,' she screeched excitedly 'it's hovering over the harbour wall.'
The tiny harbour was dotted with stranded boats at low tide, but today the tide was in and they bobbed around merrily like plastic ducks.
'Hurry up Sammy,' I urged. 'We need to get on the wall so we can see what they're looking for.'
'How d'you know they're looking for something?' she retorted. 'They might be just flying around.'

38

'Because it's obvious,' I said crossly. 'Now hurry up!'

The harbour wall was a few feet above us now and we climbed the steps eagerly and started running towards the entrance. The helicopter had moved a few feet but was still hovering, but something else was happening too.

'Look,' I exclaimed. 'There's a man coming down on a rope. They must be rescuing someone. I'm going up the steps over there so I can see better.'

'Wait for me!' Sammy cried.

But I shook my head sternly. 'It's too dangerous,' I said firmly. 'Wait here and I'll tell you what's happening.'

As soon as I got to the top of the wall it was obvious what had happened. Floating in the sea, his arms thrashing around wildly, was an old man. He must have been fishing off the wall, I thought, at the same time spotting an abandoned rod. I wonder what made him fall in?

'There's a man in the water,' I shouted down to Sammy. 'They're trying to rescue him.'

'Why did he fall in?' Sammy shouted back. But at that moment we both got our answer as a big gust of wind lifted me off my feet.

'Come down Mickey!' Sammy screeched. But I was already on my way. The rescue was exciting and I wanted to see it, but the sea looked very cold and rough and I didn't want to fall in.

Sammy and I stood there watching until the helicopter disappeared from sight. The old man was winched in safely, to applause from the gathering

39

crowd, but everyone was drifting off now, and the
harbour was returned to the seagulls.

'What shall we do?' asked Sammy, obviously keen
to continue our adventure. But my eye had been
caught by an injured sea bird so I motioned her to
be quiet.
'It's hurt its wing,' I whispered, urgently. 'Run and
get Mum and tell her to bring a box.'

******

It was 12 o'clock by the time I woke up and for a
moment I hoped it had been a dream.
'You there, Das?' I whispered to the silent room.
'I'm going to put the kettle on.'

I could hear seagulls from the flat, the familiar
sound, mixed in with the traffic momentarily lifting
my spirits. But then I heard a siren, its wailing noise
reminding me of a few hours earlier, and in a split
second death crowded in again.

I had some tea and several fags, the fags tasting
horrible to my morning palate, but then I was
hungry so I searched the fridge.
The police will be here soon, I thought, finding
nothing worth eating. I can't even go out.

I could hear the rain again so I opened the curtains
to look. Thank fuck I've got the flat, I thought, but
for how long?'

I switched on the telly, hoping for escape, but the
choices were cooking or news and the news was
depressing. I needed something to do to take my
mind off things. I'd look for a phone charger.
Everyone had a Nokia charger. That was a well
known fact.

I felt bad ferreting around the flat, the remnants of
Das's life a sad reminder of the pointlessness of it
all, but my search was fruitless and strangely I felt
relieved.

The bang on the door made me jump and I opened it
carefully, hoping it wasn't one of Das's friends.
'Mickey Spiller?' asked the copper, pushing past me
to dodge the rain. 'I need a statement, mate.'
'Sure,' I replied. 'Come in.'
My statement didn't take long as I didn't know
much, but PC Blake was in no rush to leave.
'A cup of tea would be nice,' he said cheekily.
'Shall I put the kettle on?'
'If you like,' I agreed, resigned to his company.
'Why not?'

In the end, PC Blake didn't stay long as a call came
through on his radio. 'Take care lad,' he said as he
flung open the front door, 'you don't want to end up
like Darryl...'
'Too right,' I confirmed to his departing back. 'I'll
be alright.'

Closing the flat door felt like the end of a chapter
and for a moment I felt completely lost. I didn't
know Das well enough to know if he had any

41

family. I didn't even know his friends. But
somehow I felt like I should be *doing* something.
What I really needed to do, I supposed, was to
contact his landlord. But that was the last thing I
*wanted* to do so I dismissed the thought quickly. It
would only be a matter of time before he found out,
anyway, and time wasn't on my side.
The phone was my major concern now, as I needed
it working to speak to Tim, so I decided to go to
Argos to see how much a charger would cost.

The rain had turned into drizzle by the time I left
the flat, large puddles in the ice damaged road the
only sign of its earlier fury. I'd found an old
umbrella whilst I was looking for the charger, but
now I felt stupid so I put it down. Umbrellas
weren't really my thing, but for a brief moment it
had made me feel respectable.

Argos was only a few minutes walk away so before
long I was browsing through the hundreds of pages,
reading descriptions of things I didn't want. There
were pages and pages of chargers with some that
claimed to suit every phone. But when you looked
closer, there was a long list of compatible phones
and the script was too small to read.
After a few minutes I found the right page and
scanned for the price. '£22.40! You're having a
laugh,' I said out loud. That would be a quarter of
my money.
I sat down on the coloured chairs flicking the pages
of a free catalogue, wondering what to do next
whilst I watched the happy looking shoppers.

After a few minutes I got up and left the shop. I had hoped for some sort of inspiration, some glimmer of an idea which would lead me to a charger, but nothing had come to mind.

The skies had cleared, leaving a grey windless day, but it still felt damp and cold and I longed for my bed.
You're just fed up. I reasoned with myself. Come on Mickey. Cheer up. But I couldn't talk myself out of it, and I could feel a blackness descending, so I decided to go for a walk.

This time I walked through the town, staring aimlessly into the shop windows as I headed up the hill. My mind was racing with the events of the last 24 hours and I really felt like having a drink, but somehow Das's death had been a wake up call and I decided not to. After a few minutes I reached the memorial and sat down on a bench. I rolled a fag and just sat there for a few minutes watching the world go by, trying to work out what to do. If I didn't have a charger my phone was useless. If I bought one I'd use a lot of my money. If I didn't buy one I could miss out on an important call from the Housing Trust. And if I somehow managed to steal one I'd probably get caught.
Reluctantly, I walked back down the hill and handed over £22.40 to Argos.

******

I caught the seagull quite easily, and by the time
Sammy came back with Mum we were almost
friends.
'We'll put him in the box and take him home,' said
Mum, taking charge 'and tomorrow we can take
him to the bird sanctuary.'
'What's a sanctry?' asked Sammy, looking alarmed.
'They won't hurt him will they?
'Of course not, silly,' I replied. 'It's a place where
they look after birds isn't it Mum?'
Mum nodded, her attention focused on trying to get
the gull's head to stay in the box. 'That's right she
said,' finally managing to close the flap over the
indignant bird. 'And after we've given them...Has
he got a name yet?' I shook my head. 'We'll have a
look at all the other birds.'
'That sounds like fun,' beamed Sammy, doing a
little dance around the wriggling box. 'Can't we go
now?'

That night I went to sleep and dreamt about
helicopters with broken wings, the events of the day
sparking a wild impossible fantasy.

I woke up early with a sense of anticipation and ran
down eagerly to check on the gull. Mum had put
him in the larder with a basin of water and some
food but I was worried about him and hoped he
hadn't died. Cautiously, I opened the door a little
and poked my head round the corner. 'Hello
Jonathan.' I whispered as my eyes adjusted to the
dark. 'Are you OK?'
*Jonathan* was sitting in the middle of the water
bowl apparently unconcerned by his new

44

surroundings. His damaged wing was draped sadly over the edge, reminding me that he was injured, but apart from that he seemed very happy.

'What you doing, Mickey?' said a curly head which had suddenly pushed inbetween my legs. 'Is he OK?'

'He's fine.' I whispered back, indicating to Sammy to be quiet. 'Look. He's having a bath!'

'Can I stroke him?' asked Sammy sweetly. But I think she knew the answer to that one because she ran off down the hall calling for mum in a loud whisper.

By ten o'clock we were in the car travelling towards the sanctuary. *Jonathan* was in his box, following a short struggle, and could be heard complaining on the back seat.

Normally, Sammy and I fought over who should sit in the front with Mum, but this time the battle field was the back with Jonathan.

'It needs to be Mickey.' Mum said firmly. 'Just in case he tries to escape.'

'I could stop him 'scaping,' retorted Sammy. 'Mickey gets all the fun jobs. It's not fair!'

'I know sweetheart,' placated Mum 'but you're better at navigating so I really need you in the front with me.'

'That's true.' Sammy replied seriously. 'I'm better at reading the maps, aren't I mummy?'

It was a beautiful day, the sky piercing blue with a few wispy clouds. Sammy was tracing our route with her finger, occasionally looking up from the map to give Mum instructions. I had a feeling that

Mum knew the way, though, as Sammy's
instructions were always a fraction after the event.
'It's up this hill,' said Sammy confidently, a few
seconds after we'd started the ascent. 'and then we
go round a corner.'
'Which way?' I teased. But Sammy ignored me,
pretending she hadn't heard.
'I think it's left,' said Mum, diplomatically. 'Does
that look right to you Sammy?'
'Yes, and there's the sign!' she said triumphantly.
'See. Mickey. I told you I was good at maps!'


******


I opened the door onto the high street clutching the
precious charger in my hand. It had begun to get
dark now, the street lights casting eerie shadows on
the cobbled pathway, people scurrying with
upturned collars and down turned heads. I was
feeling quite depressed about spending so much
money, but I knew that I'd made the right choice.
This was the new Mickey. Theft wasn't on the
agenda.
I walked up the hill in the failing light, my feet
feeling heavy and tired, grateful yet again for the
key in my hand.
Inside the flat it felt gloomy so I turned on all the
lights. Nothing had changed since the morning as
no one was there but me, but somehow I felt like I
was being watched.
I'd bought some food on the way home, carefully
seeking out reduced items on the supermarket

46

shelves, so now I went into the kitchen. I put the food in the fridge, leaving out the stuff to make a ham sandwich, and plugged the charger into the wall.

'Das, mate. You there?'
The voice was coming from the letterbox and was accompanied by a bang on the door.
'Come on Das. It's cold out here,'
Shit! I thought. What should I do? But it was easiest to do nothing and after a while the banging stopped. I don't know why I was so afraid. After all, I was there with Das's consent. But now that he was dead things had changed, and the last thing I wanted to do was to talk to his friends. I'd hardly known him. It just wasn't right.

## DAY FIVE

I woke up early the next day aware that my time in
the flat was probably coming to and end.
The phone had been charging for hours now and
showed a full battery so I switched it on cautiously,
hoping it wouldn't go mad with messages.
The last time it had been on had been the night
before I was arrested so there should be some. But
*bad news* had a habit of travelling quickly in my
little community so it would probably be alright.

BEEP BEEP, BEEP BEEP,  it went for what seemed
like ages, but there were only 6 messages and none
of them mattered anyway.

It had only been two days since I went to
Eastbourne, so I wasn't  expecting to hear anything
from the advice centre, so when the phone rang an
hour later I was really surprised.
'Hello.' I said cautiously to the alien device. 'Who's
calling?'


******


'Hello there,' said a flustered looking woman in her
mid forties. 'We're not open yet. What have you
got?'

'It's a bird and he's hurt,' said Sammy taking
charge. 'So you'll have to let us in won't you?'

48

'Don't be rude Sammy.' I whispered. But I needn't
have worried because Mum pulled Sammy behind
her and started to explain.

'He's still a baby,' said the red faced woman 'I
expect he hurt his wing learning to fly. It happens
sometimes, particularly if it's windy.'

'It was very, very windy,' piped up Sammy.
'Mickey nearly got blown off the wall!'

'What wall?' asked Mum sounding alarmed. But
luckily I was saved by *Jonathan* who was
squawking noisily at being handled.

'There there, my *loverly,*' crooned the woman softly.
'Let's find you a nice warm bed.'

'What will happen to his wing?' I asked as we
hurried along behind the woman who seemed to
have sprouted wings herself.

'They'll have to pewtate it,' said Sammy
knowledgeably. 'I've seen it on television.'

'I think you mean amputate,' laughed the woman
kindly, 'But don't worry. I'm sure the vet will be
able to fix it with a splint and when he's better we
can let him go.'

'What's a splint?' asked Sammy determinedly. But
at that point Mum took charge again and told
Sammy that she'd explain later.

Jonathan was released from his box into a nice
clean aviary. He hopped out gratefully, shook as if
to say 'thank goodness for that' and headed straight
for the food tray.

'That's right, *loverly.* You have a good feed now
and I'll come to check on you later. Would you like
to look around?' she asked, turning back towards us.

\*\*\*\*\*\*

'Mickey, it's Tim from Eastbourne Housing Advice.
I've got some news for you.'

A few minutes later I put the phone down and
exhaled loudly. There was just a chance that I'd get
some temporary housing!
Tim explained that he had submitted my application
for re assessment and pointed out that I shouldn't
have been deemed intentionally homeless when I'd
last applied.
'I'm waiting for a call back,' he'd added 'and if
they agree you'll need to go to the accommodation
tonight.'
'You've no idea what good timing this is.' I'd told
him, briefly explaining what had happened to Das.
'I'll be waiting for your call.'

The rest of the day dragged. I put the phone on the
windowsill in the kitchen where the signal strength
was best and spent most of the day checking that I
hadn't missed a call.
By 4 o'clock I'd given up hope and was thinking
about going out for a walk. The clock on the kitchen
wall ticked loudly, seemingly determined to remind
me that time was short. But the phone remained
silent and a cloak of depression was beginning to
envelope me. Why couldn't things go my way for a
change? I mused, resignedly. Why was it always so
difficult?

By 5 I knew it was too late so I got the phone from the kitchen and threw on a coat.

It was getting dark outside and the temperature was dropping rapidly. I'd better get used to it, I thought, I'll be back on the streets soon.

'Is Das in?' asked a voice from the shadows as I opened the door. 'I've been trying to ring the bastard and his phone's always off.'

'Err no,' I replied cautiously. 'You haven't heard then?'

'Heard what? He hasn't been nicked again has he? I told him he wouldn't be able to stay out of trouble.'

'It's a bit worse than that.' I replied gently, figuring that he had to be a friend. 'You'd better come in.'

******

On the way back form the bird sanctuary Sammy babbled non stop. 'I want to be a vet now,' she announced as soon as we got in the car 'and then I can save lots of animals.'

'Thought you wanted to be a dancer.' I sneered impatiently. 'You'll have to work really hard at school if you want to be a vet.'

'I can do that, can't I mummy?' replied Sammy confidently. 'Mrs Blackshaw says I'm intelligent.'

'She doesn't know you then, does she?' I retorted nastily. But Mum was stopping the car and I knew I was in trouble.

'That's enough Mickey,' she said sternly. 'Leave your sister alone. You can both be whatever you want when you grow up.'

51

'Sorry.' I mumbled almost inaudibly. 'I'm hungry.'
'You're always bad tempered when you're hungry.'
observed Sammy in the most grown up voice she
could muster. 'Daddy said so the other day.'
'No I'm not.' I retorted. But she was right and I
knew it.

The rest of the journey passed in relative silence
and before long we were back at the cottage, our
argument forgotten..

'What shall we do this afternoon?' Mum asked as
we sat down in the little sitting room.

******

Das's friend was clearly shocked. He slumped
heavily into a chair when I told him the news, and
three cups of tea and about ten fags later he was still
there.
'I've known him all my life,' he explained when I
gave him tea number one. 'I just can't believe it.'
It was beginning to get dark outside so I got up to
close the curtains and just then the phone rang.
'Hello..' I said cautiously, hardly daring to hope.
But for once my luck was in and apologising
profusely I ushered Das's friend out so I could pack
my stuff.
'I'm really sorry mate,' I said as I closed the door
'but I have to go soon and I need to leave the place
secure.

'Sure...' he said still looking a bit shocked. 'see you around.'

By the time I'd got my stuff and locked up the flat it was 6 pm. For a moment I wondered what to do with the key, but I reasoned that the Landlord would expect it to be inside so I left it in the kitchen. No going back now, I thought as I closed the front door. But I was glad, and as the door clicked shut I felt a weight lift from my shoulders.

Tim had given me the address of my new temporary *home* a B & B in Eastbourne, but I was under no illusions that it would be a nice. I had stayed in these places before, and the best that you could say was that you had a roof over your head. Better than the streets though, I reminded myself firmly, and perhaps a stepping stone to something more permanent.

By 7.30 I had arrived at the address and was signing the contract with a worn out looking man in his mid fifties.
'You have to be in by eleven and stay the night every night,' he sounded bored 'and if you don't, we report it to the council, and they evict you. I don't make the rules he said,' obviously expecting me to complain 'but I do have to enforce them, so don't go thinking you'll get round me if you mess up cos you won't.'
'I *won't* mess up.' I reassured us both. 'This is the best thing that's happened in ages.'
'Glad to hear it lad,' he said softening slightly.
'Here's your key and I suggest you read the

53

contract. It's at the top on the right by the way...'
And he disappeared into his dingy office, returning
to the flickering and somewhat outdated TV.

My room was as small as I had expected, but the
first thing I noticed with gratitude was that it was
warm. On the left hand wall as you walked in was a
radiator followed by a rickety looking wardrobe
with a single bed opposite. I shut the door quietly,
as if to say 'Welcome Home' and walked the ten
steps between the bed and the wardrobe to the
window. Much to my surprise and pleasure, I could
see the sea, and for some time I just stood there
staring with fascination at the rooftops and then the
sea itself. 'You've landed on your feet, Mickey,' I
murmured to myself quietly. 'Things are looking
up.'

# DAY SIX

I slept well despite my new surroundings and for the first time since my release I woke up feeling relaxed.

The room was a bit stuffy after a night with the window closed, but I was warm and dry and the place was surprisingly quiet.

I'd pretty much collapsed with exhaustion the night before, hardly bothering to get properly undressed, but now I was desperate for the toilet so I pulled on my jeans and headed cautiously to the bathroom.

The bathroom was shared by several rooms and predictably left much to be desired in the way of cleanliness, but the lock on the door worked and it was private, and after a few months sharing a cell it was heaven.

The bathroom consisted of a shabby looking avocado coloured bath, a toilet with a lime scale problem, and a scummy looking sink and mirror. There was also a rather sad, limp looking shower head dangling from the bath taps, but I figured it was more for washing hair than showering as there wasn't a curtain.

'Hurry up mate!' said a slightly desperate voice from outside. 'I had a vindaloo last night if you know what I mean.'

'Just coming mate,' I replied, noisily flushing the toilet and blowing my nose, 'I know exactly what you mean!'

When I got back to my room I had a proper look round, hoping to find a kettle. The wardrobe door

55

was hanging open, the catch no longer catching anything, but the shelves inside were intact, and before long I had filled them with my scattered belongings.

It's a good job I haven't got much, I mused whilst fiddling with the catch. I'm not sure it would stand the strain!

I found the kettle eventually – it was on top of the wardrobe behind a spare pillow – but there was no sign of anything else so I sat down to make a list of essential shopping. I wouldn't be able to cook as there wasn't a cooker, but there was plenty I could do with cold food once I'd worked out what to buy.

Despite the lack of facilities, I was feeling more optimistic than I had for some time, and a short while later I padlocked my door and went downstairs to explore my surroundings.

The building was Victorian and had probably once been a large fashionable town house, but somewhere along the line it had been converted to B&B and now it was more of a hostel.

At the bottom of the stairs, just before the front door, was a sliding glass panel with a bell on a shelf. 'Office' announced a torn paper sign.

'PLEASE RING BELL'

'Good morning,' I said to the woman behind the glass 'Do I need a key for the front door?'

'You have to ring the bell if you want something,' she replied without looking up 'and then wait until I'm free.'

'But you are free...' I glanced at the newspaper she
was reading. 'That's why I didn't ring it.'
'Rules are rules,' she retorted briskly without
looking up from her paper. And she continued to
ignore me until finally I pressed the bell.
'What do you want?' her head shot up from the
paper 'You're new I suppose.'
And I repeated my request for a key.

As it turned out a key wasn't necessary as the
'office' was manned 24hrs by at least one person
and late comers were let in providing they had a
good excuse.
'And make sure you're back by 11,' she said to my
departing back, 'or we'll have to inform the
council.'
'Will do.' I replied mildly, determined not to be
rattled by her rude manner. And I opened the front
door and walked down the steps into the sunshine.

The house was in a tree lined residential street in
what looked like a reasonable part of town, and as I
strolled towards what I thought was the town centre,
I found myself nodding good morning to anyone
who looked my way. 'Lovely day, isn't it?' I said to
an old lady who had replied to my nod with a smile.
And I meant it.
My shopping list wasn't long as I had very little
money now, but knowing that I needed to be careful
I decided to explore a bit before I bought anything. I
had been to the town on several occasions, mainly
for Court or Community Service, but I didn't really
know it, and now that I was a resident it was taking

57

on a different personality. I live here, I thought happily. This is my home.

******

That afternoon Sammy and I played in the harbour. The morning at the sanctuary had been fun and we'd enjoyed the drive, but now we were eager to explore the village, and before that the beach.
The tide was fully out as I went down the weather worn steps to the drying sand below and Sammy, who had run ahead, was already playing in a rivulet.
'Why's there still water here, Mickey?' she asked curiously. 'Come on, we can build a castle and let it flow into the moat.'
'It's coming from a storm drain,' I said knowledgeably, not admitting that I'd asked dad the day before. 'You build a castle Sammy. I want to look at the boats.'
'They're boring,' she retorted as she started to dig a hole in the sand, 'but I don't need your help anyway so you can go and see them.'
'Thanks.' I muttered sarcastically. 'Let me know if you get stuck.'
'I won't,' she said confidently, 'I'm good at building castles. Daddy said so.'

The boats were attached to ropes or chains, most of them half buried in the still wet sand, and for a while I amused myself by digging them out and following them as far as I could to where they were anchored. But soon something else caught my eye and this was much more exciting.

'Whathaveyoufound?' shouted Sammy, uncannily aware of my discovery. 'Bring it over here!'
'I've got to dig it out first,' I snapped impatiently. 'Get on with your castle and I'll show you when it's free.'

At first glance my find was rather ordinary, but as I gently dug the bottle out of the sand my excitement increased. I was right. There was something inside it.
'What is it?' asked Sammy who had been unable to resist her curiosity. 'Is it a treasure map d'you think?'
But I was concentrating hard on my excavation so it was a few moments before I replied.
'I expect it's just a bit of rubbish.' I said, trying to sound bored so she'd go away. But I was excited and I think she sensed it so I gave up and decided to involve her.
'I'll try to open it when the bottle dries,' I said in a businesslike manner, 'otherwise it could get wet when I pull it out.'
'That's what I thought, too,' she was trying so hard to sound grown up, 'Can I hold it?'

****** 

When I returned with my shopping there was a note pinned to my door. 'Ring the housing office,' it scrawled. 'they need more information.'

Alarmed, I put the shopping down on the bed and dug my phone from my pocket. Here we go, I thought, I knew it was too good to be true. But as it turned out they only wanted to know the date I came out of prison.

'We'll be in touch when we've assessed you,' the housing officer said when I'd given him the date. And before I had a chance to say anything else he was gone.

Thank fuck that was all he wanted, I thought. But the call had rattled me and it was hard to regain my earlier feelings of optimism. I could be chucked out at any time, and I'd be back to square one. Until they agreed to house me that was just a fact of life.

For the next couple of hours I just sat and thought about what to do if I got thrown back on the streets. But nothing I thought of was really practical and by the time I'd finished imagining myself living in an abandoned beach hut, I'd arrived at a calm acceptance.

The truth was that there was very little I could do other than hope. If I was thrown back on the streets I'd have to deal with it, but for now I could enjoy having a home. Home, I thought looking around at the bare walls and shabby furniture. My cell had been more homely by the time I'd finished my sentence and at least I'd had a TV. I'd have to try to get a community care grant so I could at least buy a radio and a few new clothes. At the moment my wardrobe consisted of one pair of jeans, two pairs of boxers a T Shirt and various odd socks!

As I was mentally composing my application for a grant there was a knock at my door. Fuck. I thought, falling quiet and hoping they'd go away. But the knocking persisted and in the end I decided to pretend that I was in bed. 'WHO IS IT?' I shouted, trying to sound half asleep. 'I'm in bed at the moment.'

'It's me mate. Steve. You know, we sort of met in the crapper this morning.'

'Oh yeah, I remember,' I replied warily. 'what d'you want mate? I'm trying to catch some sleep.'

'Let me in and I'll tell you,' he insisted. 'I can't tell you through the door can I!'

I was rather hoping that he wouldn't tell me at all, but he didn't seem dangerous so I ruffled up the bed cover, kicked off my trainers and slowly opened the door.

'I've got some gear to sell,' Steve said as soon as he'd plonked himself down on the bed, 'd'you want some?'

'No thanks mate.' This was just what I didn't want. 'I'm being tested,' I lied. 'I just can't risk it.'

'You on licence then or something?' he asked sullenly. 'It's really good gear, too.'

'It's a long story,' I replied evasively, 'but cheers for asking. I'd have bitten your hand off a few weeks ago, but for now I just can't.'

'You got any friends that might want some?' asked Steve persistently, beginning to sound a bit desperate. But this time I simply shook my head and yawned.

'alright mate,' he gave up. 'But if you change your mind I'm in number 12.'

'Thanks.' I replied stifling another yawn whilst ushering him out of the door. 'I won't forget.'

******

As soon as the bottle was dry I gingerly tried to unscrew the lid.

'Come on,' said Sammy impatiently, 'it can't be that hard.'

'I don't want to break it, do I?' I snapped back.. 'If I twist it too hard the top of the bottle might snap.'

'I don't think you're strong enough,' she challenged. But I wasn't falling for it so I decided to ignore her.

After a few minutes of gently working the lid from side to side it loosened suddenly and I unscrewed the rest easily to the accompaniment of claps from my excited sister.

'I'm sure it's a treasure map,' she whispered in my ear, 'we'd better watch out for pirates'

'Yes.' I replied, deciding to play along. 'I think we need to post a look out just in case. You'd better go and stand by that rock and whistle if anyone's coming.'

When Sammy reached the rock I waved to her and indicated that she should keep her eyes open and look around. The bottle was completely dry now and the paper inside beckoned to me like a Xmas present but I studied it first to work out the best way to get it out undamaged.

62

'There's a man and a dog coming,' shouted Sammy anxiously. 'Hurry up Mickey,' she urged. 'He looks s'picious to me.'
'He's probably just walking his dog.' I said meanly. And I turned my attention back to the bottle.

******

When Steve had left I sat on the bed and rolled a fag whilst I thought about his visit. It was important to keep things sweet in a place like this but at the same time I really wanted to stay off the gear. It was the same in prison really, but the consequences of upsetting someone there could be much more serious so on balance I decided that I'd nothing to worry about.

For the rest of the day I just sat and thought. Things were OK for the moment and so far I'd managed to keep my head down, but I knew that the chances were that I'd get kicked out soon and the state of limbo was depressing. What I needed to do, I decided, was to go for a run and blow away some cobwebs.

By the time I went out it was getting dark, but it was warm enough and for a change there wasn't a breath of wind. I didn't have a track suit or any proper running shoes, so everyone I passed seemed to stare as if something was wrong, but by the time I got to the seafront I was immune to them. The sea was flat calm, the tide a good distance out and overhead was a cloud of starlings swirling around like a swarm of gigantic bees. The fresh air and

running had lifted my mood, but I was unfit and out of breath, so as soon as I could I found a bench. 'In memory of Clive and Milly,' it said 'and the many happy holidays they spent in Eastbourne.'
I rolled a fag with slightly cold hands, swearing as some of the tobacco blew away. But for now nothing could depress me and I sat there contentedly, relishing the feeling of the smoke rolling off my tongue..

After a while I got up and ran home, the orange street lights casting friendly shadows as I sped along the abandoned pavements. I'm happy, I thought cautiously. But don't count on it Mickey. Don't count on it.

When I got back there was another note pinned to my door.
'Police are after you,' it stated menacingly. 'you need to go to the station and ask for DC Hood.'
There you are, I thought, almost pleased that my prophecy of doom had come true. I told you it couldn't last, and I went downstairs to reception to see if they knew any more.
This time, I rang the bell and waited patiently.
'Yes?' said another bored looking staff member.
'What d'you want?'
'There was a note on my door saying that I need to contact the Police.' I replied as politely as I could. 'I just wondered if you knew what they wanted and if it was urgent.'
'Oh it's you is it? he replied, suddenly a bit more interested. 'I don't know what you've done lad but

64

they're very keen to talk to you. You'd better get down there now.'

'Didn't they tell you anything?' I persisted. But his eyes were back on the TV and I sensed that I'd been dismissed.

'I'm going out then,' I said to the back of his head. He didn't even grunt.

The Police Station was about a half an hours walk away so I had plenty of time to think, but I knew that I hadn't done anything so I wasn't too worried. They probably just wanted some more information about Das, I reasoned, and by the time I got there I was feeling pretty confident.

DC Hood was short, fat and the wrong side of fifty. 'Thanks for coming in,' she said briskly. 'Come through.'

'Do I need a solicitor?' I laughed nervously. But she shook her head and ushered me into an interview room.

'You're not under arrest,' she reassured, 'but I do have a few questions for you about Darryl.'

'I thought it might be that.' I relaxed slightly. 'Well at least I couldn't think of anything else it could be. But I hardly knew him really.'

'Could you go over the night that you found him,' she asked casually. But somewhere in my head an alarm was starting to ring and for a moment I said nothing.

'I gave a full statement.' I pointed out firmly. 'I really don't have anything to add.'

'Yes, but it would really help if I could hear it from you first hand,' she encouraged. And deciding that I had nothing to lose I told her how I found him dead. 'So how do you account for the large amount of your finger prints in his bedroom? she asked tonelessly. 'They were everywhere.'
'I think I'll have a solicitor now,' I replied without blinking, 'and I won't answer any more questions till he gets here.'

By the time the duty solicitor arrived it was ten pm, and despite the stress of my situation I was yawning my head off. As soon as I'd elected to have a solicitor, I'd been formally arrested on suspicion of murder, and taken to a cell where for two hours I'd stared at the ceiling cursing my luck.. My finger prints were bound to be all over the room, I'd stumbled around in the dark looking for a towel, and I must have touched loads of things. Did I say that in my statement? I wondered. But I couldn't remember, and if I hadn't it would seem like I was making it up. Fucking hell….. This was serious!

******

I shook the bottle gently, and after a few seconds the note was in reach of my finger tips. The paper was perfectly dry and only slightly discoloured but I was worried it would fall to bits. I dug it out gingerly, trying not to tear it, and after a few

66

seconds I was holding it between my finger and thumb.

'Aren't you going to open it?' piped Sammy who had appeared at my elbow.

'Don't rush me,' I replied, 'it might tear or fall apart.'

But the truth was that as long as it was folded up it was a mystery with limitless possibilities and I didn't want to spoil it.

'Promise me you won't try to grab it or anything,' I said seriously.

Sammy, nodded her curly head, showering us both with specks of sand, and for once convinced that she was taking me seriously, I sat down, gently clasping the note in my shaking hand.

At the top of the note was a date written in longhand, but I couldn't quite make it out so I jumped down a line, keen to read further.

'*IF YOU FIND THIS PLEASE RING Halland 66279 for further instructions*' It said 'and ask for Trevor Bell.'

'That's boring,' remarked Sammy as she jumped up and ran back to her sand castle. But I hardly heard her because I was studying the date with disbelief. The note was dated 2nd September 1902!

When we got back to the cottage I showed the note to my Dad.

'It looks genuine to me,' he said seriously. 'Look at the phone number. That's how they used to be when the exchange was still quite small.'

'But how can we ring it? I asked. 'It won't exist any more will it?'

'Not in that format,' he replied, 'but it might be possible to trace who it belonged to if we go to the library. It could take quite a while because you'd have to go through the old phone directories, but I think it would be possible.'

'I think I'd find that fun,' I affirmed. 'It would be like being a detective, wouldn't it? Like in that book you used to read us.'

'Do you mean 'Emile And The Detectives?' Dad laughed gently. And I nodded, already lost in the adventure to come.

\*\*\*\*\*\*

The solicitor didn't make me feel much better. 'They've got enough to charge you,' he stated resignedly, 'but a lot will depend on who we get for the interview.'

'I know.' I said, helplessly. 'And knowing my luck it will be a Rotweiler,'

'Are you sure you don't have anything else to tell me?' he asked for the third time. But there really wasn't anything else to say. I'd been there and my prints were in his room. What mattered now was my original statement.

The taped interview was with DC Cole as DC Hood had gone off shift. DC Cole was about thirty, already balding, and he looked bored.

'Taped interview with Michael Spiller,' he announced as soon as we'd sat down. 'Also present are DC Cole, Investigating Officer, and Richard Hughes, duty solicitor.'

'Before we answer any questions I would like to have sight of my clients original statement.' Richard stated firmly. 'And I then might need to confer with him again in private.'

Whilst Richard was reading my statement I stared around the room hoping that I was giving the impression that I had nothing to worry about.
DC Cole sat opposite me, his hands on the table, a pen neatly placed on a blank note pad. I smiled at him in as friendly a manner as I could manage, but I knew that he was my adversary and this was a game of nerves.

'My client admits to being in the deceased's room prior to the discovery of his body so I'm not sure what it is that you are concerned about.' Richard said quietly. 'He was staying there with the permission of the deceased.'

'Can you prove that you had his permission?' DC Cole addressed his question to me. I looked over at Richard uncertainly.

'I'm going to recommend that my client answers no comment until we have had another opportunity to discuss matters alone,' said Richard, picking up on my uncertainty, and to my surprise DC Cole agreed to a short adjournment.

'Interview suspended at 10:55 pm,' he said, turning off the tape. And he left the room, leaving us on our own.

'He seems reasonable,' remarked Richard, 'but unless you've some way to prove that you were staying at the flat with Darryl's permission we could be in a tight spot.'

'There were lots of his friends round the second night I was there,' I said unhappily, 'but they were stoned and I've no idea who they were. The only other thing I can think of is that I told the guy from Eastbourne Housing Trust where I was staying.'

'Was that before Darryl died?' asked Richard searchingly.

I nodded. 'Definitely.'

I gave Richard Tim's details, even somehow dredging up the phone number, and we banged on the door to let them know that we'd finished.

'My client can prove that he had the right to be at the address, Richard announced triumphantly. He came here of his own free will so he clearly isn't a flight risk. He'll be willing to comply with any conditions of bail you impose.'

'OK. Well it would seem prudent to check that out before we go any further,' acquiesced DC Cole. 'Interview terminated at 11:15 pm.'

By midnight I was bailed and free to go. The only conditions imposed being that of residing at my current address and signing on daily, neither of which was a problem. What was a problem, though, was that I was now late and would have to face the wrath of the 'B & B' night staff.

The night was cold now and I shivered as I walked along the deserted streets, but I knew I was lucky to still be free. I'd been remanded in custody for much less.

'Who is it?' growled a voice from behind the chained door. 'You're late.'

\*\*\*\*\*\*

After finding the note in the bottle the rest of the holiday seemed to drag. It was still fun, don't get me wrong. I loved hearing the gulls and playing by the little boats whilst Sammy attempted to build castles. But all I really wanted to do was to investigate that phone number.

We got home a couple of days before the end of the summer holidays, the days already shortening and the buzz of school in the air. I was keen to get straight to the library, my quest to solve the puzzle feeling quite urgent. But Mum had other plans for us, and for 2 unbearable days we were dragged around the shops buying our school stuff.
Why does everything have to be new?' I complained. 'We were only at school six weeks ago and it was good enough then!'
'It just has to be,' replied Mum firmly, 'because it has to last for another year.'
'I like it,' Sammy piped up, whilst looking at Mum for approval. 'Can I have a fluffy pencil case?'
But Mum was focused on her tightly held list, and she didn't reply until Sammy asked again, by which time the effect of having sucked up had worn off.

'We'll see,' Mum replied vaguely as she ushered us into the underwear department.

The first day of the new term was fun as we hadn't seen our friends for a few weeks and there was a general sense of chaos as everyone got used to their new timetables. I'm going to the library today, I thought excitedly, by tonight I could know who wrote the message.

When school ended at three thirty I almost ran out of the gates.
'SLOW DOWN!' shouted one of the teachers at my disappearing back. But I was through the gates now and stopping for nothing. The library was only open till five. I'd have about an hour.

******

'I'll have to report you as late,' grumbled the receptionist as he opened the door to me. 'you'll probably get kicked out.'
But I didn't reply. I'd save my excuses for someone more influential. All I wanted to do was sleep.

## DAY SEVEN

I didn't wake up until ten, and for a moment I felt
quite good, the night before still buried in my
memory banks. But within seconds it all came back
to me and I stared at the wall in disbelief. I was on
bail for murder!
It was about as bad as it could get.
'You in there?' The voice was accompanied by a
persistent knocking. 'I've got the housing on the
phone.'
'Why didn't they ring my mobile?' I asked
grumpily. But as I felt around for it on the floor I
realised that it was probably dead.
'You coming, or what?' insisted the voice, 'I would
if I were you.'
I heard his footsteps descending the thread bare
stairs.

Hurriedly, I pulled on my jeans and a T Shirt, and
barefooted, I ran down the stairs.
'He's here now,' announced the receptionist handing
me the phone with an undisguised look of disgust at
my bare feet. 'and get some shoes on when you've
finished.'

'I'm afraid I've got some bad news for you,' said
the nameless Housing Officer. 'We've assessed your
case thoroughly and you are not considered to be in
priority need.'
'What does that mean, then?' I asked, already
knowing the answer. 'How long have I got?'

'We'll give you 48 hours to move out,' he sounded apologetic, 'but if you don't you'll be evicted by the Police'

'Thanks for nothing,' I retorted angrily slamming down the receiver. And if I hadn't already been in trouble, I might well have punched the smug looking receptionist as well.

'You gotta leave then.' He didn't even try to hide his pleasure. 'Make sure you leave your room tidy.'

\*\*\*\*\*\*

As soon as I got to the library it became obvious that the task in front of me was massive. Dad had told me that there weren't so many people with phones when the note was written, but as I stared at the rows of directories I wasn't so sure.

'Is there a way to find an address from a number easily?' I asked the prim looking librarian.

'Check the pre fixed areas first,' she whispered, 'that will cut out quite a lot.'

By the time the library was closing I had only gone through about twenty pages, but somehow the search was fascinating. So many people…So many lives…I thought. I wonder where they all are now?

'You'd better come back when you've got more time,' advised the librarian unnecessarily. 'We're open until 4 on Saturdays.'

On the way home I thought again about my treasured note. What did it mean? Who was it from? Where might it lead?

******

I spent the rest of the day staring at my bedroom wall. Not only was I homeless again and on bail for murder, but I would soon be in breach of my bail conditions. I might as well give up.

At about four I reluctantly plugged my phone in to the charger, turning it on as I did. 'You've missed four calls from 0775678…..' the message bleeped at me, and as I sort of recognised it I rang it back.

'Tim speaking.' He sounded tired. 'How's it going at the B&B?'
'They're kicking me out and on top of that I got arrested for murder.' I replied despondently. 'I really don't know what to do.'
'So that's why the police called me last night.' He sounded more awake now. 'Have they charged you with anything?'
'Not yet,' I replied, 'and before you ask, I didn't do it. I'm bailed to this address, though, so I don't suppose I'll be your problem for much longer.'
'I'll have a think and ring you back.' He tried to sound upbeat. 'But I can't promise anything.'
'I realise that,' I said 'but thanks for trying. I appreciate it.'

'Don't give up just yet,' he advised. 'I'll ring you in the morning.'

*Don't give up.* I echoed to the room. But giving up was just what I felt like doing. Mentally I was already back in prison.

## DAY EIGHT

Although I didn't sleep well, I woke up feeling a bit more positive. Just for a change I hadn't actually done anything wrong and I felt sure that time would prove me right. If Tim could come up with somewhere to live it was only really a matter of notifying The Police of my change of address so they could vary the bail conditions.

I made some toast and a cup of tea, and got back into bed to wait for the call.

By noon I wasn't feeling so confident, but right on cue the phone rang and it was Tim.

'I've got you into a night shelter,' he said triumphantly. 'You normally have to wait until 6 to see if they've got any beds, but I used to work there and I pulled a few strings!'

'When do I need to be there?' I asked excitedly. 'What's it like?'

'It's not great,' he admitted, 'and you'll be in a dormitory. But it must be better than custody or the streets and you can go tonight.'

'Thanks, Tim.' I said warmly. 'I won't forget this. Can you text me the details?'

By 5.30 I'd gathered my stuff and was waving goodbye to the surly receptionist. 'Your room better be clean,' he shouted after my departing back. But I ignored him. I was sad to move out because at least I'd had some privacy, but the staff left a lot to be desired and I was hoping that the hostel would be more friendly.

The hostel was only a couple of miles walk, so by 6.30 I was checking in. 'You get a locker so you can keep your stuff safe,' said the volunteer behind a shabby looking wooden desk, 'and I advise you to use it.. We don't accept any responsibility for things that go missing here, and believe me they do!'
'I haven't got much, anyway.' I tried to sound sad. 'But I'll lock up what I've got so don't you worry.'
'Good,' she smiled, 'you're in room 3 and dinner's at 7.'
'I haven't got any money for dinner,' I stated. But she shook her head.
It's included in the rent,' she told me. 'They'll adjust your benefits.'

******

When I got back from the library there was a Police car outside my house. That's odd, I thought as I opened the front door. I wonder what they want.

## DAY NINE

The first night in the hostel was noisy but OK, and
by seven I was up having breakfast.
'You have to go out for the day,' I was advised by
my key-worker, John, who had appeared at my table
from nowhere. 'It's the rules, I'm afraid.
'So long as I can come back,' I replied resignedly.
And he nodded his head and went through all the
hostel rules.
'Once you're here, you get priority,' he explained,
'but if you're not back by 6 your space could be
given to someone else.'
'Don't worry, I will be,' I assured him. 'I've got
nowhere else to go.
'Good,' he replied. 'I'll leave you to find your feet
today and tomorrow we'll do all the paperwork.
'What paperwork?' I asked. But I had already
guessed, so I zoned out and didn't listen to the
answer. I would have to change my housing claim
and benefits again. I would probably end up with no
money.

After speaking to John, I got my stuff for the day
and went out into the cold crisp morning.
Number one on my list of things to do was to
inform the police of my change of address, and
number two was....well there wasn't a number two.
With no money, no local friends and a murder
charge hanging over my head I seemed to lack
motivation.

******

The first thing I noticed when I opened the door was that the place was brightly lit. That's unusual, I thought, They're usually really careful with the electricity.

'Mum...,'I shouted, surprised that she hadn't appeared when I opened the door. 'Where are you?' But instead of Mum there was a strange looking lady.

'You must be Mickey,' she sounded sad. 'Come and sit down, lad, I've got some difficult news.'

'What's happened?' I asked with a sinking feeling. 'Where's Mum?' But somehow I'd already guessed the answer, and when I went into the sitting room my worst fears were confirmed.

'There's no easy way to tell you this, Mickey,' said the strange lady. 'I'm afraid your parents have been killed in a car crash.'

'But they can't be,' I stammered, 'Mum doesn't go out in the car without Dad and he's at work.'

'I'm so sorry, Mickey,' she said sadly, 'but I'm afraid it's true. They were in the car together and they both died at the scene of the accident. These Police Officers can confirm what I've said and they've already spoken to your sister.

'Where is she?' I asked desperately. 'Why isn't she here?'

'She's been taken to some foster carers,' she explained, 'but don't worry, you're going to the same place so you'll see her soon.'

'I don't want to go into foster care!' I shouted, hot tears filling my eyes. 'I can look after Sammy here. It's MY house.' But even as I spoke the words, I knew that they would never allow it.

******

Changing my address with the police proved simpler than I'd expected so I had the rest of the day to think about how unlucky I was. I'd only been out less than two weeks and I was on my third address and back on bail. Surely things would have to look up now, wouldn't they?
I thought about going to the job centre and looking for a job, but for that I would need a better address than the night shelter, and anyway what was the point? Until I knew what was happening with the murder charge the whole of my life was basically on hold.

It was cold now, though still bright, and the clouds were scudding along at quite a speed so I suppose it was windy, but I couldn't feel it. Unable to think of anything else to do, I walked slowly towards the seafront, noticing as I did that I was looking at my feet. Come on…I tried to gee myself up. It's a mistake, you'll be cleared. You haven't done anything.
'Spare any change, mate,' asked a well fed looking street drinker, 'for a cup of tea.'
'I wish I could,' I replied honestly, but we're in much same boat I reckon.'

'Fair play,' he replied as I walked away. 'Good luck, mate.'

******

I don't remember much about the first few weeks after the accident, but I do remember trying not to cry but ending up sobbing. Sammy and I were staying with a middle aged couple until they found us something more permanent and they were OK, I think, but I can't really remember. To be fair, nobody would have been good enough so they were probably nice. I just wanted my parents back..
 On the first night, Sammy had cried herself to sleep in my arms, her hair matted and soggy from so many tears, her little arms wrapped round my neck. I did the same myself once she was safely in bed, but with no one to hold and nothing but my dark thoughts to keep me company, the loneliness was unbearable.

The *plan* according to the social worker was for a long term foster placement to be found for Sammy and me, a family who we could *bond with* a family that would *meet our needs*. And for a while we were busy working out what sort of family we wanted. We thought it would happen quickly as it was mentioned so often, but weeks turned into months and months blurred into the following year, and soon we forgot we were going at all.
We were still at the same school (this had been considered important by those that now ran our

lives) but now we were *in care* and everyone from
the caretaker to the mums and dads that hovered
outside at the end of the day, knew.
Most of my friends had been nice, some even
inviting me to tea a few times. But nothing was
helping me to feel better, and I hated the sympathy,
and every time I saw someone whispering I thought
it was about me.

'It'll take time for you to get over it, Mickey,'
advised the social worker one day when she picked
me up from school. 'You'll feel better then, I
promise.'
But I didn't feel better, and I doubted that I ever
would, and now when she said stuff like that I could
feel myself getting angry.
'How do you know it will get better?' I retorted
crossly on one occasion. 'I bet your parents didn't
die, did they?'

After a few months we got a visit from the Family
Placement Team who wanted to know everything
from our favourite colours to whether or not we
liked cats.
'I want a swimming pool,' piped up Sammy,
excitedly, 'and horses too.' she added.
'We'll see what we can do,' laughed the fat lady
with the red face and clothes that seemed too big.
'Who knows...'
But I didn't miss the glance that was exchanged
between them when they thought I wasn't watching,
and I could feel my ears burning with anger.
'Have you thought about being adopted?' asked the
one with the terrible haircut and bright red finger

nails. 'Did Jenny discuss it with you, because if she
didn't we could run through it now?'
'We don't want to be adopted,' I said quietly. 'We
had parents.'
'OK,' she said, sounding relieved, 'it would have
been difficult, anyway.'
'How long's this going to take?' asked Sammy,
already riding her horse around the swimming pool.
*Haircut* shook her head. 'It's impossible to tell,' she
replied, 'because we want to try to match you to the
best couple available and that takes time.'
'I don't care what they're like if they've got horses.'
Sammy announced, firmly. 'I just want a horse.'

Over the next few weeks we asked about moving
every time we saw the social worker, but the answer
was always the same.
'No news yet, I'm afraid. It takes time. We'll let you
know.'


******


By the time I reached the promenade the wind was
blowing a gale. For a while I just stood there
watching the seagulls battling the wind. But it was
too cold to stand still for long and the wind was
pushing me on, so with the day stretching in front of
me I started to walk. The promenade was mostly
deserted, the wind deterring all but the most hardy,
but I felt invigorated and alive, and for a few
minutes I almost forgot my problems.

'Watch out mate!' I shouted at a skateboarder as he narrowly missed my foot, but the words were snatched by the wind and he didn't even look up. I used to enjoy skateboarding, I mused, remembering the first one I'd had and the never ending fiddling with cold fingers and reluctant wheels. There was less traffic then, and you could sometimes skate the length of a road without having to stop, but you still got shouted at, that hadn't changed.

'How did it get to this?' I shouted loudly into the wind. Life had seemed simple once, the future beckoning like a good friend. But the answer was out of my reach, lost in the cries of gulls, and soon, my mind wandering off at a tangent, I had forgotten the question.

After a couple of hours I was so cold that I had no choice but to return to the relative warmth of the town. It was still too early to go back to the night shelter, but at least it was getting dark now so it would only be a couple of hours. How does anyone do this for more than a few days, I wondered. I'd been on the streets for short periods, and that was bad enough, but having to wait in the cold to get in for the night was awful!

As I walked past Primark I glanced in through the well lit windows and spotted a warm looking coat. I wish I was wearing that, I thought wearily, pulling the collar of my jacket up to try to cover my neck. It was bloody freezing.

'You window shopping, Mickey?' asked a vaguely familiar voice from just behind me.

'Sam!' I exclaimed as I wheeled round. 'What the hell are you doing here?'

'Shopping, mate,' he replied with a twinkle in his eyes. 'You look freezing!'

'I am,' I admitted. 'This coat's not much good but it's all I've got at the moment. What are you shopping for?'

'Anything I can sell on.' He laughed. 'Do you want me to get you a coat?'

'I'd love you to, mate,' I replied sincerely, but I can't afford to get into any trouble at the moment.'

'I'm not nicking the stuff,' He laughed. 'I buy all the sale items and ends of line and sell them at the market. It's a nice little earner!'

'Bloody Hell, Sam. I never thought I'd see the day. What happened?'

'I got fed up with always looking over my shoulder,' he replied seriously, 'and I was always being bloody caught!'

'That's my thinking now too mate,' I said wearily. 'But I'm not sure how long it's going to last, cos everything keeps getting fucked up.'

'Sounds like you could do with a beer and a chat..' he invited. 'Come on. Let's get out of this fucking weather!'


'To be honest, Sam, the weather is really the least of my concerns right now,' I announced once we were sitting in a warm pub with a warm pint. 'By this time next week I'll probably be on remand for murder.'

'Fucking hell, Mickey!' He sounded genuinely shocked. 'That's a bit heavy mate. What happened?'

'Well I didn't do it, for a start,' I stated, firmly. 'But I'm not sure that that will make any difference. I was there, you see, and there was no one else.'

Over the next two pints I spilled out the whole story, carefully going over it in my own mind with each sentence I spoke.
'But that's just circumstantial,' Sam finally commented. 'They've go nothing, mate. You'll see.' But I heard the doubt in his voice despite his reassurance, and for a while we just sat there, nursing our drinks.

'What you need right now is a bath and a place to stay.' Sam announced, still looking at his beer. 'Come on mate, I'll put you up for a while.'
'Are you sure? I asked, hesitantly. 'It's just that once I leave the night shelter it will be difficult to get back in.'
'I know,' he stated calmly, 'I've been there, mate. You can stay till you get back on your feet. I'll enjoy the company.'

****** 

Life in foster care soon became familiar, and after a while I got used to all the meetings and events.
'It's important that you come to the reviews,' I was told by one of our social workers, when I asked if I could just stay at school instead. 'It's important that you feel involved in all the decisions about your future.'

87

'I can't see the point,' I retorted rudely. 'You just do what you want to do, whatever I say.'
'That's not fair, Mickey,' she replied without conviction, 'we always listen to you...'
'Well why haven't we got a permanent home yet then?' I asked for the hundredth time. 'It's always set as an aim in these meetings and never happens. I'm fed up with not knowing where we'll be next week.'
'Come to the meeting and tell them just that,' she smiled.
And I realised that I'd fallen into her trap.

At the review we were introduced to yet another reviewing officer who pretended that he knew all about us.
'Are you happy with the plan, Mickey?' he asked after they'd gone through the previous plan and noted what had and hadn't happened.
'What plan?' I said sulkily. It's the same as last time. All you do is talk.'
'Well I like it,' piped up Sammy who must have heard the word horse or something, 'and I want a biscuit.'
'So we're all agreed,' stated the reviewing officer. 'Mickey and Sammy are to remain with the Clarks until a long term placement can be found.'

After that they set the date of the next meeting and everyone left hurriedly, keen to beat the rush hour traffic.
Nothing had changed.

On the way home the Clarks chatted enthusiastically about the meeting apparently

88

pleased that we were staying, and for a minute or two I allowed myself to feel pleased too. At least we knew where we were for the moment, even if that moment might be brief.

'It's not so bad with us, is it?' questioned Mrs Clark brightly.
We both shook our heads.
'It's not that we don't want to stay with you,' explained Sammy diplomatically, 'it's just that we don't know how long we'll be with you or where we'll be going to next.'
'I know, dear,' she sighed, 'but we'll just have to make the best of it. Why don't we bake a cake when we get home?'
'Only if I can do it all myself,' replied Sammy, the conversation drifting back to normality, 'and Mickey can lick the bowl.'

******

Sam's flat was much bigger than I'd expected and I was pleased to see that I could sleep on the sofa without having to curl up my legs.
'Make yourself completely at home,' he'd said generously once he'd shown me where everything was. 'I'll be out at the markets quite a lot but you should have everything you need.'
'It's brilliant, mate,' I smiled. 'I won't forget this.'
And that was that.

That evening Sam and I reminisced about some of
our shared experiences and even, as it turned out,
one shared girlfriend. Despite this lucky turn of
events though, I felt low. History had taught me that
my luck didn't last very long and with the spectre
of a murder charge lurking in a well lit corner of my
mind, it was difficult to think otherwise.
'Have you got a good brief?' Sam asked when the
subject cropped up again. 'Only, I know someone if
you haven't.'
'He seems pretty sharp,' I sounded slightly
uncertain, 'but I'll bear that in mind, mate. Thanks.
For now I just hope it's all going to go away.'
'Me too,' he sympathised. And we changed the
subject to happier times.

I had known Sam on and off since I was at school,
but it wasn't until I did my first spell in a YOI that I
really got to know him. At the time, being sixteen
and full of bravado, I had thought it almost funny to
be imprisoned, but as soon as I'd arrived at the
Young Offenders Institute I'd changed my mind. On
the outside I'd considered myself to be quite *hard*,
but in there my petty crimes and short sentence
made me a little fish in a very big pond.
'You better watch yourself.' A thick necked, shaven
headed boy of about seventeen announced in the
first association. 'This is my wing, *Blood*. Don't you
forget it!'

'Do you remember that hard nut with the thick
neck?' I asked Sam, knowing that he would. 'I heard
that he died last year, stabbed up by a rival gang.
Couldn't have happened to a nicer person, could it?'

******

Life had returned to normal at the Clarks, one boring emotionless day seeping into another, but all of a sudden something seemed wrong.

'It'll be fine, love,' I heard Mrs Clark reassure Mr Clark when she didn't know I was listening, 'they're good with cancer now.'

Oh great. I thought, immediately feeling guilty at my lack of compassion. That's all we need. But for a while nothing much happened and I assumed that he had got better.

When the change came it came out of the blue, Sammy and I returning to find Mrs Clark in tears being comforted by our social worker.

'I know I'm being silly,' she blinked back her tears. 'and plenty of people survive these days. But I just can't do everything,' she said. 'How quickly can you arrange respite?'

'By tomorrow, I hope,' replied our social worker looking at me sympathetically, 'I'll talk to the children whilst you make a cup of tea. Could you go upstairs and get Sammy for me Mickey,' she added. 'I'll explain what's going on.'

Neither Sammy nor I slept much that night. The social worker had explained that they were looking for an emergency placement for us as Mr Clark had undergone major surgery the day before and would be ill for some time. But she couldn't say if we'd return to the Clarks', and suddenly it seemed important that we did.

'I like it here,' announced Sammy sulkily. 'Why can't we just stay here and help? I could do all the cooking.'

'It's just not possible, I'm afraid,' came the whispered response, 'Mrs Clark needs to focus on her husband.'

The next morning we were due to go to school but Mrs Clark kept us off.

'They are coming to get you later,' she explained with a sad smile. 'They've found you a family on Wickstead Road.'

'But that's on the council estate,' I objected. 'It's rough round there and we'll hate it.'

But she wasn't really listening, and anyway I knew there was nothing I could do so I shut up. The Clarks, I suddenly realised, had been OK.

By lunchtime we were packed and ready, and had said goodbye to our rooms. Sammy was excited as she'd decided that this was just a holiday, but I was worried and knew that we wouldn't be coming back. Mrs Clark was doing her best to reassure us that only *nice* families were allowed to foster children. But we were going to Wickstead Road. Why would anyone *nice* live there? I knew children from Wickstead Road at school and they were about as far from who I wanted to be friends with as you could get.

For Sammy's sake I tried to put on a brave face, even suggesting that our *holiday* might be fun. But inside I was dying again. This could not be a change for the better.

The social worker arrived in her shiny car at about two and we said our goodbyes to Mrs Clark. I shook her hand as dad had taught me to and thanked her for all that she'd done for us. Sammy hugged her and said that she'd make a cake at the new place to give to Mrs Clark when we came back.

Now sitting in the back of the social worker's car, I was even more sure that we would never return. I waved to Mrs Clark as we pulled away and closed my eyes for a while, listening to Sammy babbling to the social worker.

Wickstead Road was just as I'd imagined it. Row after row of identical looking houses stared out of it, their scruffy front gardens totally visible through metal fencing. Every few gardens there would be a fridge or a sofa sadly adorning the neglected lawn and I counted at least three cars without wheels, their bodies suspended like dismembered corpses on piles of sun bleached bricks.
'Nearly there,' chirped the social worker. 'It's number 103. They're a lovely family with a child of their own so you'll have a friend to play with.
'What!' I exclaimed, totally unprepared for other children. 'I don't want to live with other kids...'
'It'll be fine, Mickey,' she replied. 'It's not forever and it was the best we could do at short notice. They are a nice family and Tom is around your age.'

'I think it will be fun,' announced Sammy, probably imagining pyjama parties. 'It will be like going to boarding school.'

'No it won't,' I sneered, unable to stop myself. But I caught a look from the social worker in her rear view mirror and shut up.

'Here we are then,' she exclaimed, pulling up outside what was clearly one of the better houses. 'Your new foster mum's name is Alice Shorecroft and she likes to be called Alice.

'What about Mr Shorecroft?' asked Sammy. 'What should we call him?'

'Tom's father doesn't live here dear,' she replied, 'but you'll like Alice. She's very nice.'

'Well, *I* won't be staying if I don't like it.' I announced truculently as I opened the car door. 'And there's nothing you can do to stop me.'

'That's true,' she replied tiredly, 'but I think you should give it a try, don't you? I know this is another big change, but it might be for the best.'

'I can't see how.' I retorted sulkily. But I knew enough to shut up, resolving as I did that I would run away if it turned out to be the nightmare I expected.

## DAY TEN

Now that I had somewhere to live the world looked a little brighter and for a while when I woke up I allowed myself to think that things would work out. It was raining outside, I could hear it splattering against the windowsill, but according to the morning news it had warmed up. Sam had given me a warm coat anyway, but it didn't look like I was going to need it just yet.

The day stretched before me with only my trip to the police to look forward to, but then I realised that I would need to change my address at the job centre. Fortunately, I didn't need to claim housing benefit whilst at Sam's, but I didn't want my Job Seekers Allowance to be delayed in any way as I was down to my last two pounds.

Soon after eleven, I ventured out into the grey day, keen to explore my immediate surroundings. It had been dark when we'd got the flat the previous night and I only had a vague idea where we were. Sam had told me that it would take about half an hour to walk to the police station so I set off in what I thought was the general direction, asking in a corner shop as soon as I found one.
'Hope it's nothing serious, love?' enquired the curious elf like woman behind the counter. But I shook my head and smiled. I would not be today's gossip.

As I walked along the rain soaked pavements I mused that it was less than two weeks since I'd got out of prison. *Inside*, days turned to weeks turned to months turned to years with little changing, but on the outside I was living from day to day with everything changing by the hour. I'd had plans before I left, plans that had seemed quite reasonable at the time. And I still wanted to straighten out if I could, don't get me wrong, but everything seemed to be against me and it was difficult to see how things would change. Sam was being fantastic, and I was very grateful to have a roof over my head, but I couldn't stay forever, and with no money and no job it would be impossible to get anywhere of my own.

When I arrived at the police station there was a queue, so I sat down on a red plastic chair next to an old lady.
'It's been a right to do, here!' she said cheerfully, her bedraggled grey hair falling over one eye. 'It's better than telly, I'd say.'
'What's being going on then?' I asked politely, not keen to talk but aware of her loneliness. 'And what's a nice lady like you doing here, anyway?'
'I've lost my cat,' she said, a tear immediately springing to her eye, 'and they said I've got to wait till they're less busy.'
'Oh dear. What's he look like?' I asked sympathetically. 'Perhaps I could keep an eye out for him.'
'He a very fat ginger Tom,' she replied fondly and his name is *Scamp*. You'll know him if you see him because he's so big. I'll give you my address.

'You shouldn't go giving your address out like that,'
I warned her, 'especially not in here.'
But she was already scribbling it down on a torn off
bit of envelope and my warning fell on deaf ears.
'If I find him I'll bring him round,' I said as I got up
to go to the counter. 'I expect he's just gone
walkabout.'
'Thanks love,' she replied, thrusting her purse into
my hand. 'Take a pound so you can ring me. He's a
bit feisty being a ginger and he might bite.'
'I don't need the money,' I lied, handing her back the
unopened purse. 'And don't you worry. I'm good
with cats. They like me.'

The next stop was the job centre where I explained
yet again that I'd moved.
'It'll probably delay your giro,' said the disinterested
advisor, 'but it might not. It's difficult to tell. You'll
have to apply for a crisis loan if it does.'
'I know,' I said, sounding as bored as she did. 'Let's
hope I don't have to.'
'Who can tell...' she replied, beckoning to the next
customer. 'It's the luck of the draw.'
On that note I turned to leave just as a fight broke
out between two drunks in the queue. What a
fucking depressing place.

By the time I got home it was mid afternoon and I
was starving. Time for a sandwich, I thought,
extracting a slightly squashed looking loaf of bread
from my rucksack. Or beans on toast perhaps.

When Sam got back at about 4 pm I was stretched
on the sofa watching daytime TV.

97

'Had a good day, mate?' he asked as he took off his coat and shoes. 'I've done well at Renton market so I thought we'd get an Indian?'
'Are you sure? They're very expensive,' I replied, secretly salivating at the thought of chicken madras. 'I can't even chip in right now.'
'It's fine, mate. I don't expect you to. Relax, will you. I've been there remember! Oh and by the way I bumped into my brief on the way home and he said to call him if you need to. Here's his card.'
I took the card hesitantly as if taking it would seal my fate, but I soon forgot about it as we ordered our takeaway and the conversation and beer flowed.
'I changed my address at the job centre today,' I explained, 'and guess what? My benefits might be delayed. Don't worry,' I added, 'I'll get a crisis loan if I have to. It just pisses me off. It's all on the fucking computer and changed in a matter of seconds. Why should it delay anything?'
'I reckon they do it on purpose, mate,' Sam replied with a smile. 'Lets get hammered!'


******


Wickstead road was awful but the social worker was right about Alice. She was really good fun.
'Come in you two,' she'd said cheerfully when we'd arrived, 'I'll show you your rooms and then we'll have a snack. I've got chocolate cake and toast. How's that sound?'
'Yummy!' Chirped Sammy already half way up the stairs, 'But Mickey doesn't like cake.'

98

'I do! I just don't like yours,' I retorted meanly. And
Alice laughed heartily, casting me a mildly
reproving look.
'I can see I'm going to have my hands full,' she
winked at the social worker. 'Tomorrow at eleven,
then. I'll go up and settle these two.'

My room, much to my surprise was large, bright
and clean. I walked in slowly glancing around at the
pine coloured wardrobe and chest of drawers and
the plain blue carpet. The bed was on the right hand
side with the head end near the window, but it was
to the window that I now went. The view from the
window was of the back garden which was neat and
quite big with a climbing frame in the middle.
Perhaps this would be OK after all.
'Come on you two. Tea's on the table,' shouted Alice
from downstairs, 'don't want the toast to go cold do
we?'
'Where's your husband?' asked Sammy, coming
straight to the point as usual. 'Is he dead?'
'Not the last time I saw him!' laughed Alice, 'but it's
a long story.'
'I like stories.' Sammy stated, completely failing to
grasp the situation. But I shushed her firmly, putting
my fingers to my lips, and for once she listened.
' I think you'll like it here,' announced Alice
brightly. 'But I'm sure it will take a while for you to
settle in. It sounds to me like you've had a pretty
rough time. Now, then, tell me what you will and
won't eat.'

******

The chicken Madras was absolutely delicious. The first decent meal I'd had since before going inside. Sam and I chatted affably for the rest of the evening, steering clear of anything depressing, and after a few beers we were both feeling sleepy.

'I'm going to hit the sack, mate,' he announced at about 9, 'I have to be up at five.'

'I can give you a hand if you want,' I offered. But he shook his head.

'You need to get your own life sorted, mate,' he advised, 'and I'm used to working alone if you know what I mean. I'll see you tomorrow.'

'Sure.' I replied with a yawn. 'And thanks mate. Is it OK if I have a quick shower?

'Of course,' he nodded, shutting the door to his room. 'Help yourself.'

## DAY ELEVEN

That night I dreamt about being in prison again. It was a disturbed dream, fantasy mixing with real memories, but it was vaguely comforting too. Prison had become familiar, and although I didn't want to **be** there it didn't frighten me like it had done when I was younger. When I was sixteen I'd only served three weeks and that had been enough to make me hope that I'd never go in again. But as my life drifted further and further into crime and I got longer sentences, I got used to it. You knew where you were in prison once you were settled on a wing, and you didn't have to worry about paying your bills.

I got up feeling slightly hung over from the previous night's beers, but after a large mug of tea and several roll ups I felt better. Sam was right. I needed to sort my life out, and this was the time to do it.
At about ten o'clock my mobile rang, and it was my solicitor.
'Just ringing to remind that you've got to answer to bail tomorrow,' he advised. 'I'll meet you there at ten.'
'Do you think they'll bail me again?' I asked. I've got somewhere better to live now.'
'Have you advised them of your new address?' he asked. 'We don't want any breaches of bail, do we?'
'Of course I have,' I confirmed. 'Do you think they might NFA it tomorrow?'

'I doubt there'll be no further action at this stage,' he replied, 'in fact I doubt that they'll have done anything much at all yet. See you tomorrow.'

The next call was from Tim who had discovered that I wasn't at the night shelter any more.
'Let me know if I can be of any more help,' he said after I'd updated him. 'But it sounds like you've fallen on your feet.'
'I think I might have this time,' I confirmed. 'Thanks for all your help, Tim.'

By the time I'd had a bath and some breakfast it was close to eleven thirty. I'd glanced out of the window earlier, and the day had looked bright and cold, so I put on the new coat for my trip to the police station. I was feeling better than I had for days so enjoyed the walk which took me past the corner shop where I'd previously asked the way.
'Morning!' I said cheekily to the elf like woman who was leaning out of the door having a fag. 'Nice day, isn't it?'
'Lovely,' she replied stamping on her fag end. 'I've got work to do.'

Glad of the coat as it was really very cold, I stepped up my pace and arrived at the police station within 20 minutes.
This time it was empty, and as all I had to do was to sign in, I was out again in about thirty seconds. I was still very worried about the murder charge, but as time past it seemed less real, and feeling on a bit of a high I decided to look for a job. For all I knew the police could drag their heels for months and I'd

be in limbo. I hadn't done anything, that was the truth, but I couldn't wait for them to agree.

The job centre was pretty busy, mainly with people with benefits enquiries, but I found myself some space and started looking. I'd done all sorts of things for short periods of time, but I didn't have any real qualifications or particular skills, so it was pot luck really. Most of these jobs were minimum wage anyway, so it was more about trying for something I could tolerate. It was the wrong time of year for the building game which would have been my preference, and I couldn't apply to shops etc. because of my record, but there would probably be something if I kept looking. There usually was.

After a few minutes I looked up from what I was doing and spotted someone I knew across the room. Fuck! I thought. He was the last person I wanted to see, and if he saw me I'd probably have to run. But he hadn't spotted me yet, luckily, so I left hurriedly, keeping my head down as I passed to his right. Having spent so much time in the local prison I knew a lot of **faces**. And for the most part that was fine. But *this* face was trouble with a capital T. And I'd hoped I'd never see him again.

As soon as I was sure that I was free and clear I stopped to roll a fag. It was windy and my hands were still shaking from the near miss, but somehow I managed it without losing all the tobacco. Fuck. That was close. I thought, drawing deeply on my fag. I need a drink!

The nearest pub was a bit of a dive and my two pounds would only buy me a half, but it was the only thing I could think of that would stop my heart

103

from pounding so I handed it over willingly to the bored looking bar maid.

'Want any crisps?' she asked as she took the money. 'They're going cheap cos they're out of date.'

'No thanks, luv,' I smiled. 'That's the last of my money.'

And I took a seat by the window, anxiously glancing around the room as if he might have got here before me. 'Get a grip, Mickey.' I admonished myself. 'For fuck sake, get a grip.'

'You can have a packet for free,' said the barmaid, launching them over the bar in my general direction, 'they'll be thrown out tonight, anyway, and they're salt n vinegar and I don't like them.'

'Thanks! They're my favourite,' I smiled at her, reappraising my earlier assessment. 'I'm bloody hungry so they'll go down well. What's your name?'

'It's a packet of crisps not an invitation to dinner,' she replied with a slight smile, 'and my name's Sue, though they call me *Razor.*'

'Why's that?' I asked curiously. 'You're not dangerous are you? I must admit that your crisp throwing was a bit aggressive!'

'Because I'm very hairy and I've always got one with me just in case,' she smiled, 'and somehow it always falls out of my bag along with anything else which could embarrass me.'

'Just in case of what?' I asked cheekily. 'You're not planning to strip off are you?'

And she laughed like a drain, her face blushing, whilst her hand went down behind the counter to retrieve another packet of crisps.

'Catch!' she ordered as the crisps flew towards the far end of my table, 'and don't be so bloody cheeky.'

104

For the next half hour Razor and I chatted affably
and I was reluctant to go back into the cold.
'See you again,' she said as I opened the door.
'You're welcome back any time. Most of my
customers can hardly string a sentence together.'
'I'll have more money next time,' I promised,
sounding more certain than I was, 'and I'll buy you a
drink.'
And with that I closed the door and returned to the
world.

As I'd blown out the job centre and didn't dare go
back, I found my self wandering in the direction of
the flat. I was skint now anyway, and it was
pointless just walking around in the cold, pretending
that I had a life. The sky looked as if it might snow
at any minute, too, and although I liked the snow,
I'd rather be in the warm watching it covering the
grey depressing streets, than *it* covering me. I heard
it was different if you were out in it somewhere
where it snowed a lot, like in a ski resort. But this
was just about as far as you could get from that and
I didn't want to get cold and wet. 'You've got
somewhere to stay.' I reminded myself. 'You can get
warm and dry.' And I sighed with the sort of relief
you can only feel if you've known the opposite.
The roads were wide and tree lined now as I got
closer to the flat, and after ten minutes or so I sat on
a low wall to smoke.
'Miaow.' Mewed a friendly looking cat who
somehow seemed familiar. And he wound his way
round my legs, begging for attention.
'Hello mate,' I said, stroking his soft ginger head.
'You're a big lad aren't you?'

After a few minutes, I stood up to leave and the cat looked at me quizzically and gently nipped my finger.

'I've got to go, mate,' I said firmly as I stroked him one final time. 'Go and get in the warm.'

After about ten paces I realised that the cat was following me.

'Go home,' I said firmly as he wound himself round my legs again. And the penny finally dropped.

'You're lost, aren't you? You're the *lost, fat, ginger cat!'*

And I scrabbled around in my pocket for my wallet, hoping I'd kept the scrap of paper.

******

'Who've we got this time, Mum? said a voice just as the front door slammed. 'They better be better than the last lot, or I'm off.'

'Stop it, Tommy,' she retorted, crossly, 'and come in properly and meet Mickey and Sammy.'

'Sorry, Mum.' He was a well built boy of about 15 with blond, unruly, curly hair. 'I was only joking.' And he bounced into the kitchen like a big naughty puppy.

'You alright?' he waved at Sammy and me. 'I'm going out again, later, you can come if you want.' And he turned on his heel and bounded up the stairs.

'Don't mind, Tommy,' said Alice with a slightly exasperated smile. 'He's a nice lad, really and I'm sure you'll all be good friends. No going out tonight though, I'm afraid. We've got stuff to do.'

'What stuff?' Sammy asked, staring in the direction of the kitchen door as if Tommy was still there. 'I think it would be fun to go out.'

'Of course it would,' I intervened, 'but we have to settle in tonight and we've got school in the morning and Alice wants to get to know us, don't you?'

Alice nodded, clearly relieved to have me on her side.

'Let's just get to the weekend,' she said, 'then you can go out with Tommy.

The next couple of days went quickly and to my relief nothing much had changed other than where we lived. Tommy didn't go to our school as it wasn't the closest and he was hardly in anyway, so Sammy and I had a chance to find our feet.

'I like it here,' Sammy announced as we were about to set off for school on Friday morning, 'and I like Alice.'

'Me too,' I agreed. But somehow I felt uneasy, as if I was waiting for something bad to happen. 'Just be careful, Sammy,' I advised as I left her at the school gates, 'not everyone's nice, you know,'

'Yes they *are*,' she retorted as she skipped towards her classroom, 'you're just a worry wart and you don't like it cos Tommy's older than you.'

'It's got nothing to do with that,' I shouted back. But her pigtail was disappearing into the room as the door closed, so I gave up and walked to *my* class, wondering if perhaps she was right.

At first break I went to look for Sammy and I found
her, as always, near the library.
'Meg says she knew Tommy at junior school and he
was always in trouble,' she announced gaily, 'but I
like him and I told her so.'
'I'm not sure, yet,' I said quietly, 'he seems alright
with us, but we don't really know him yet, do we?'
'I do,' she insisted. And I decided to let it drop.
Sammy was clearly impressed with Tommy and
although I was uneasy, nothing bad had happened
and he'd been quite friendly.
'Don't forget to meet me at the gate after school,' I
reminded her as I walked away, 'you mustn't walk
home on your own.'
'Stop nagging,' she replied as she ran towards a
group of giggling girls. 'I'll see you later.'

The rest of the day passed quickly, though it did
drag a bit during double maths, and Sammy was
waiting where she was supposed to be so we set off
towards our new home chatting about our friends
and their lives.
The walk was a bit longer than we were used to, but
the weather was OK and I was happy to listen to
Sammy's chatter.
'Look at that bird,' she said, pointing to a rather
large crow. 'He's almost as big as that one in Wales!'
'I can't believe you remember that!' I exclaimed.
'You were almost a baby then!'
'Well I can,' she retorted, 'I can remember
everything we did with Mum and Dad.'
And quite unexpectedly, she burst into tears.
'It's OK.' I reassured her, gently pulling her curly
head to my chest. 'I miss them too. But we can't go

back to those days, and that's just that. Do you
fancy a race?'
She nodded, tearfully, a smile doing battle with her
sadness.


****** 


According to the crumpled piece of paper that I
eventually found in my wallet, the cat was called
*Scamp*
'Scamp.' I called, watching for a reaction. 'You're
Scamp. Aren't you!'
*He might bite you.* I remembered the old lady
saying. But Scamp was as good as gold and when I
picked him up he purred all the louder.
'We'd better get you home big fella,' I said, surprised
at his weight, 'before my arms fall off.'

To my surprise, Scamp stayed happily in my arms
until we arrived at a small Victorian town house
with shabby blue curtains.
'This is it, Scamp,' I announced as he started to
struggle a bit, 'let's hope she's in.'
There wasn't a door bell, just an old fashioned
knocker, but Scamp was scratching at the door by
now and I could see a shadow through the frosted
glass panels.
'SCAMP!' she exclaimed as the door opened and he
shot past her wool stockinged legs. 'Where have you
been? I've been so worried! And thank you so
much,' she said turning to look at me for the first

time. 'You're the man from the police station, aren't you?'

I nodded. 'It must have been fate because he almost seemed to find *me*,' I grinned, 'and he let me carry him like a baby!'

'He bit my husband's chin once,' she smiled at the memory, 'and he hit his head on the wall behind the sofa as a result. It was the funniest thing I'd seen in years..... Anyway, come in for a cup of tea and some cake, young man. It's the only way I can thank you, I'm afraid, but I'm a pretty good baker if I say so myself and the tea's already brewing.'

'That would be great.' I replied, genuinely. And the door closed behind us with a welcome thud.

I ended up spending a couple of hours with Dora as she was good company and her cake was amazing. She'd had an interesting life, particularly during the war years when she delivered spitfires to the ill fated crews of the RAF, and her house was full of all the memories that go with a life well spent.

'My husband died four years ago,' she told me sadly, 'and I miss him everyday, I really do. But Scamp's a great comfort to me, and he's so naughty that he makes me laugh so I can't thank you enough for finding him.'

'It's been a great pleasure, Dora,' I said, meaning it. And I walked to the front door somewhat reluctantly, pulling my collar up against the inevitable cold.

'Make sure you keep him in for a bit now, won't you,' I said as I stepped onto the grey street.

She nodded. 'Don't you worry, lad, he's not going anywhere.'

And as if to prove the point, she cradled him more firmly in her arms and stroked his large ginger head.

By the time I got back to the flat the wind had picked up so much that there was litter flying around the street. I wouldn't want to be out at sea in this, I mused as I walked the last fifty feet. And I wouldn't want to be on the streets.
 Inevitably, this line of thought got me thinking about my current situation again and for a few minutes I felt a bit depressed. I was lucky to have somewhere to stay and a friend to help me out, I knew that, but I needed to make a life not borrow someone else's and that's where I seemed to get stuck. If the police cleared me of involvement with Das's death then I reckoned I'd have half a chance at making it this time. But the weight of that investigation was bearing down on me like a tonne of bricks and after my near miss at the job centre I was feeling less sure. I was too well known in this area by both my peers and The Police. I wondered if my past would ever let me be free.
'Stop moaning, Mickey.' I admonished myself. 'It could definitely be worse.'
I need a nap. I thought, lying down on the sofa and flicking on the telly. That cat was bloody heavy!

******

When we got home Alice was in the kitchen baking a cake.

'Can we have some as soon as it's ready?' asked Sammy eagerly before she ran up the stairs to her room.

'Only if you help with the washing up.' Alice shouted up the stairs. 'Which reminds me. We need to sort out the chores.'

'What chores?' I asked warily as I stared at the huge pile of ironing that I'd just spotted on the kitchen worktop. 'I'm no good at ironing. I burn everything.'

'Well it's just as well that you won't have to do it then isn't it?' she smiled. 'I just mean things like taking the rubbish out and brushing the stairs.'

'Could I do some gardening?' I asked sheepishly. 'I used to do some with my dad.'

'Of course you can,' she sounded pleased, 'would you like your own vegetable patch? You'll have to wait till spring to do most of the planting but the soil's good here so I reckon you could get a good crop.'

'That would be fantastic!' I enthused. 'When can I start?'

'How about right now?' she replied getting a ball of string from a kitchen drawer. 'Let's go and mark out a plot.'

\*\*\*\*\*\*

By the time I woke up it was dark and the local news was on the telly. I stretched my legs over the end of the sofa as one of them had pins and needles and blearily watched the moving images. The clock on the kitchen wall was just visible from where I

112

was lying, and to my surprise it was 10:30 pm. This wasn't the early evening news. I had slept for hours. Probably all that cake, I thought, reasonably. But then I remembered the bottle of wine that I'd found under the sink, and my memory returned in full.

It wasn't as if I actually *needed* a drink. I could remember arguing with myself. But a glass of wine would be nice and after all I had rescued a cat, hadn't I?

Shit! I thought. I hope he won't mind. It might've been for something special. Shit!

## DAY TWELVE

Sam was fine about the wine which was fucking lucky as I had no money to replace it.

'You're welcome to anything here,' is all that he'd said. But I felt bad anyway and determined to replace it as soon as I could. When you are in prison your possessions become everything, and taking from someone else was the worst possible crime, yet here I was, less than two weeks out and I was doing it again. alright, it wasn't really stealing, more like borrowing really, but it worried me that I'd taken it with so little thought. It really did.

'I'll get you another bottle as soon as I get my benefits.' I reassured him. But he waved his hand dismissively and pretty soon afterwards he went to bed.

It was 8 am now and Sam had left soon after five for another market. I admired him immensely as he'd been where *I* was, and now he was earning a living. But it seemed like very hard work to me and I wasn't sure I had his determination.

Ahead of me stretched another fruitless day of waiting for my benefits and signing on at the police station, but I really didn't know what else to do. I could go back to the job centre and have another look, but in my heart I knew that it was pointless. As soon as they knew about my record I'd be out of the running, and that meant I wouldn't even get an interview. My only real option was to wait for the building game to pick up or go back to what I knew best and clearly wasn't very good at...

At about ten I left for the police station. The wind had calmed down but was still blowing and as I left it started to sleet. Fucking great.. I thought miserably. I'd be getting wet and cold again.
I walked briskly to keep out the cold and had decided to run back once I'd signed on as I was getting really unfit. I had worked out inside and had left feeling in shape, but it was much harder to keep it up on the outside and I certainly couldn't afford to go to the gym.

I stood in a queue of three waiting for what seemed like an eternity, but then, when I gave her my name, she excused herself and said she'd be back in a minute. Alarmed, I tried to look round the corner of the counter to see what she was doing, but I didn't need to wait long as an internal door sprang open and suddenly I was in handcuffs.
'What the fuck's going on?' I shouted as I was pulled into the custody suite. 'What have I done?'
'I'm arresting you on suspicion of Burglary,' stated the officer. 'You do not have to say anything.......

******

My garden was about ten feet square and over the next few months I worked at it tirelessly until it was something I was proud of. Sammy and I had settled in well with Alice and Tommy, and despite my earlier concerns about him nothing bad had happened. We didn't see much of him if truth be told as he was always out with his mates or playing on his X box. He invited me to play with him on one occasion, but I was useless at it having never had one of my own and he didn't ask me again.

Alice was consistently nice and we had everything we needed. But I didn't really feel like I knew who I was any more and after I'd made the mistake of telling my social worker how I felt, I found myself going to counselling.

'You're still grieving,' she said at the end of our first session. 'Give it time, Mickey and you'll feel better.' But I didn't feel better, though I pretended to so I could stop seeing her, and before long I was looking for other ways to feel better.

'Come out with me and the lads.' Tommy suggested one day when he was in a particularly good mood. 'Come out and have some fun.'

Over the next few weeks I spent more and more time with Tommy and his little gang of friends. He was right. I did have fun, and at the beginning it all seemed pretty harmless, but gradually, as the weeks turned to months we progressed from stealing the odd chocolate bar from the corner shop to stealing clothes from the shops in town.

At first I was uneasy about stealing as my father had been very strict and if I'd ever taken anything without asking I'd experienced his wrath, but this was different as we didn't get caught, and gradually I relaxed.

'Don't ever tell Sammy.' Tommy warned me the first time I went out with him. 'She will blab for sure and then we're all mincemeat.'

'I won't. I promise.' I replied solemnly. And I never did, though months later something happened which made me regret it.

******

For most of the day I had languished in a cell at the police station racking my brains trying to work out what I could possibly be accused of, but I hadn't done anything, and I had no idea what was going on.

At about four o'clock, just as I was considering trying to sleep the time away, I was taken to an interview room for questioning. I had rung my brief as soon as I'd been allowed to, and he was sitting at the table looking bored.

'I'll need some time alone with my client,' he stated firmly. And the officer left, the door locking behind him with a soft click.

'They've got fingerprints, Mickey. Why so careless?'

'I haven't done anything,' I protested. 'There must be a mistake. What am I supposed to have done?'

'They're alleging that you broke into a house and stole a sum of just under £200 in cash from a Mrs Evans,' he replied, watching my face closely. 'Your prints were on all over the place, Mickey. It might be better for you if you cooperate.'

'It's impossible,' I replied angrily. 'They must be fitting me up. I haven't done anything. But you're right. I will answer their questions because the last time I gave a *no comment* interview I got a heavier sentence. I'm not holding my hands up to something

I didn't do though,' I added. 'It's not fucking fair. This time I'm innocent.'

'It's your call,' he said, clearly not believing me, 'but if you change your mind it might go in your favour. It's not a lot of money and the victim was out so there are no aggravating factors.'

'But this is what I do, isn't it,' I said, knowing that I'd be refused bail, 'So it won't make a lot of difference whether I did it or not, will it? What else have they got?'

'Nothing, as far as I know, we won't get full disclosure at this stage unless they ask you questions that enlighten us. Our position as I understand it from you is that we are not guilty of burglary, and as long as we maintain that position they will be guarded. Are you ready?'

'Yep.' I nodded tiredly. 'Get him in.'


I was questioned for the next hour and as I didn't have an alibi for the period concerned - I think I was asleep in the flat - I was charged. The fingerprints were only on a discarded purse it turned out, not all over the place as they had earlier indicated. But I didn't recognise the address or even the road so I was at a complete loss.

'You'll be up in the morning,' The Officer said as he locked me back in the cell. 'I suggest you think carefully about your plea.'

'I haven't fucking done anything,' I retorted angrily. But he had already banged me up so I doubt that he heard.

## DAY THIRTEEN

I slept fitfully that night on the hard cell bed, but I'd already resigned myself to a slightly more comfortable bed in Prison and soon I'd have plenty of time to sleep. With my record and my short period out before I re-offended the chances of The Court giving me bail was zero. Added to which, I was still in the at risk period from my last sentence as I'd been released half way through so there was little point in even trying. We *would* try of course because sometimes the magistrates were reluctant to remand. But I wasn't holding my breath. Oh, and yes, then there was the murder enquiry...I was sure that would somehow get a mention if only behind closed doors.

The van arrived to pick me up at 9 am and as it was only fifteen minutes to the Court I had plenty of time to sit and wait.

At 9.45 my brief came down to see if I'd changed my mind about the plea, but I wasn't going to admit to something I hadn't done, and I think he was starting to believe me.

'You always hold your hands up when you get caught, Mickey,' he mused, 'but they've got fingerprints.'

'I know, but I didn't do it,' I said adamantly. 'Something's not right here.'

'OK. Well I suggest we don't indicate a plea today and opt for Crown Court. Perhaps something will come to light in the months before the trial or you may get lucky with the Jury.'

'Not with my luck,' I sighed. But he was right. Juries were all different and some didn't like to convict.

******

When Sammy came running into my bedroom in the middle of the night I thought she'd had a nightmare. She was sobbing uncontrollably, her hair all twisted and wet from her tears, and I imagined she'd dreamt about the accident.
'It's alright, Sammy. It was only a bad dream.' I reassured. But she was clearly traumatised and I had to hold her in my arms for a few minutes before she could speak.
'Ttommy hurt me,' she blurted out between sobs, 'and he told me not to tell but I *have* to.'
'What did he do? I asked. Thinking he'd pushed her or something. But the question had set her off again and then Tommy came into the room.
'She's lying,' he shouted. 'She's a fucking liar. What's she said? I never touched her, I swear.'
He was furious. 'Your sister's a little liar.'
But Sammy was calmer now and somehow Tommy's presence helped her to focus and from the safety of my arms she pointed into her pyjama bottoms.
'He touched me down there and it hurt,' she said 'and then he played with his thing.'
'What?!' I exclaimed. 'You'd better not be making this up Sammy. This is *really* serious.'

But I could tell from her face that she was telling the truth, and Tommy had bolted down the stairs and was unlocking the front door.
'I'll kill him!' I shouted as I ran after him. I'll fucking kill him! But Tommy was long gone by the time I got downstairs, and now Alice had appeared and was standing on the landing looking confused. 'What's going on Mickey? she asked urgently. 'It's the middle of the night.'


******


By eleven thirty it was all over and I was back in the Court cells waiting for transport.
My brief had made a bail application citing all the reasons that I could be bailed without risk, but we all knew it was a formality and it took the Magistrates less than a minute to decide to remand me in custody. I elected for Crown Court as we'd agreed and the next date was set for the committal. 'My client would prefer to be produced for the committal hearing rather than appearing by video link,' he informed the Court. And that was it. I was going back.
'I'll come to see you if I find anything out,' he mouthed as they cuffed me and led me out of the dock. 'Ring me.'

It was several hours before the van arrived to return me to prison, but I'd been here so many times before that I simply went to sleep.


121

'Not even two weeks, Mickey.' I'd said to myself as
I was drifting off. 'Not even two fucking weeks.'

By five o'clock I was in my cell and the last two
weeks might never have happened.
'Back again, then,' commented the reception officer.
That's a record even for you I'd have thought.'
'And it wasn't even me this time,' I said, not
expecting to be believed, 'I've been fitted up.'
'Sure you have, lad!' he said as he handed me my
bedroll. 'You and the other 650 in here!'

My cell was on a different wing this time and
initially I was glad as I really didn't want all the
questions. But after a few days I asked if they could
move me to my old wing. I had friends there, and
that was the best position to be in. Prison didn't
scare me like it had when I was younger. I had spent
so long inside that it was really my home. But like
all homes, there were rules and it was important to
be *in* with the prisoners who controlled the wing.
I've no doubt I could have worked my way in on C
wing with a bit of time. But A wing was my natural
territory so it made sense to move.
'You'll have to wait until there's a space in a
smoking cell.' The Senior Officer advised me. But I
knew it wouldn't be long as prisoners were moved
all the time, many of them to other prisons.
'Thanks Sir,' I said, nodding that I understood. 'Oh
and by the way, the TV remote's not working in
C104.'

\*\*\*\*\*\*

I'll never forget that night as long as I live. Alice
had called Social Services who had called The
Police, and within minutes, it seemed, Sammy and
the duty social worker had been whisked off to a
special unit in the Police Station.
'I want to go with her.' I argued when they'd told me
that I couldn't. 'She's my little sister. She needs me.'
But I knew that I was wasting my breath, and within
half an hour I had packed my belongings and was in
a car with another duty Social Worker.
'We've found you an emergency placement, just for
tonight,' he explained as soon as we were on our
way, 'and tomorrow we'll look for something more
long term.
'What about Sammy?' I asked tearfully. 'Will she
come too?'
But he didn't really know how long she'd be with
the police so he wasn't able to tell me much.
'You'll be back together as soon as possible,' he said.
'We always try to keep siblings together so don't
worry.'
'What'll happen to Tommy?' I asked. 'Will they lock
him up?
'I honestly don't know,' he replied, 'but he's only
sixteen so the law will protect him too. The
important thing is that Sammy is safe now, That's
what really matters.'
'I know.' I agreed. But she should have been safe
before, shouldn't she? Why did this have to happen?
It's all so unfair.'

'It's life,' he sighed, 'and, yes. It's not fair. But you'll get through this Mickey and life will go on. It always does. For now you just need some time to get over the shock. It's a cliché, I know, but it's really true. Time *really* does heal.'

That's not how it seems to me. I thought. But I didn't want to see a counsellor again so I kept quiet.

## MONTH ONE

Life in prison resumed all too easily, and days slipped into weeks with hardly a murmur. I got the occasional letter from my solicitor and Sam came to visit and tell me that he'd look after my stuff, but other than that nothing happened.

I'd been moved back to A wing within a couple of days and the prison grapevine had done me the favour of announcing my return, so after a few hours, when I got the odd comment, it was as if I'd never left.

'Thought you were staying out this time,' they said when they saw me for the first time. But most had been in the same position time and again so I wasn't hot news.

'I didn't fucking do it.' I said to one or two of my closer friends. But I doubted that even they believed me and before long I stopped mentioning it at all.

After a few weeks I got a letter from my solicitor advising me that the police had confirmed that they were taking no further action with regard to Das's death, but even that news didn't cheer me up much. This was my third burglary charge and if I was convicted I'd be looking at a long stretch under the *three strikes* rule. I had to face it and get on with my life in prison. Anything else was fantasy.

One of the things that did change with this acceptance of my fate was the way I would spend my sentence. All my previous sentences had been less than two years so I'd counted the days to my release rather than planning how to spend my time in prison. But this time I'd have time to do something really meaningful, and it was to this that I now put my mind.

Of course I'd also have the sentence plan made by Probation and this time I'd probably have to do the thinking skills programme, but there'd still be plenty of time for me to learn a trade or something and I knew that I would need to make a decision about this soon as once I was sentenced they would likely move me to another prison.

'Bricklaying or plumbing mate. That's where the money is if you get qualified,' advised one of my mates. And he was right, I knew he was, but now that I was looking at a future in prison I wasn't sure I could be bothered.

'I might go down the education route, mate,' I responded. 'I left school at fifteen when I went to a Young Offenders and I've never even taken an exam.'

'Whatever,' he said, clearly having switched off when I said education. 'You coming to the gym today?'

******

Sammy was at the police station for most of the night but at about 5 am she was brought to join me at the emergency placement.

'Go to bed for a bit,' I gently suggested once we were on our own. 'You'll feel better when you've slept and then we can talk.'

126

'I don't want to talk any more,' she said firmly, 'I want to forget it.'

And with that she went up to her room, somehow not the sister that she had been only yesterday.

'I'll be just next door if you need me,' I offered. 'I'm going to lie down but I'll be there if you need me. Get some sleep now.'

That afternoon our normal social worker turned up and we were taken to a less temporary placement. 'This isn't long term,' she announced as we were parking outside another faceless terraced house, 'but you'll probably be here for a few weeks whilst we look for something more permanent.

'I don't suppose they've got a horse?' said Sammy with a surprising attempt at humour. 'That's never going to happen, is it.'

And with that we got out of the car and knocked on the door of our new *home*.

## MONTH TWO

It was always a waiting game before you were
convicted, but this time was worse because I knew I
was going to get a long sentence and I knew I was
innocent.

I went to the gym almost every day and this helped
my anger and frustration, but something inside me
seemed to have lost hope and for the first time in
my life I knew real despair.

I was a fighter, I had had to be, and normally I
bounced back pretty quickly, but the injustice of this
was weighing so heavily that I couldn't shift it.

It's difficult for anyone who hasn't experienced it to
know how powerless you are in prison, but it was
this that I felt more keenly than anything else. I'll
admit that there were plenty of crimes for which I'd
never been caught, and I'll admit that on balance I
probably deserved the sentence I was about to get.
But I hadn't committed *this* burglary and there was
nothing I could do.

Normally, my head would be full of plans about
how I would make it work on the outside, how this
time it would be different. But now all I could think
about was the crime itself. How could my
fingerprints be on something I hadn't taken? Were
the police fitting me up because they couldn't get
me for murdering Das? Why couldn't I have had an
alibi? Why? Why? Why?

I spoke to my solicitor about once a week in the
hope that he might have dug something up. But the
reality was that he probably wasn't digging at all,
and locked up in prison there was nothing I could

do. The next time I as due in Court was for the matter to be committed to the Crown Court, and that date was fast approaching and I knew that if I wanted a lighter sentence it would be better if I pleaded guilty thus saving the tax payer from the expense of prosecuting me. But I just couldn't do it. It wasn't right, and from there I got to thinking about all the wrong things that I'd done.

\*\*\*\*\*\*

The stealing had started with Tommy and to begin with had been little more than a challenging game, but it was so easy that in the end I stole whenever I needed to, and by the time I was eighteen I needed to all the time.

I was introduced to heroin quite early in my prison career and to begin with it was fantastic. But addiction set in so fast that soon I just needed a fix to feel normal.
'You're stuck with it for life now, mate,' one of my friends had told me, 'you might as well accept it.'
But I didn't accept it. And every time I got out I tried to stop. Inside, it didn't seem to matter and it certainly helped to pass the time, but each time I got out I was determined to get clean and build a life and after several failed attempts, I did.
Now, though, I was tempted to start again and the wings were awash with the stuff. But something kept me from giving in and as I lay in my bed

thinking, I realised that it was anger. Since the death
of my parents life had dealt me a pretty rough hand,
and I'd made it worse by the life that I then chose,
but *this* was unfair and I was fucking angry. So
angry, in fact, that I was having trouble sleeping.
'You should see the quack,' one of my friends
advised, 'get some sleepers or something.'
But I didn't want any fucking pills. And I didn't
want to lose my anger, and health care was a
fucking waste of time, anyway.


******


Sammy was very quiet for a few weeks and for a
while I thought she'd never be herself again. But she
was seeing a counsellor who she got on well with
and gradually she seemed to return to normal. We
didn't discuss what had happened. Neither of us
wanted to. But occasionally we were forced to face
it again as Tommy had been charged and there was
going to be a Court Case.
I often thought of Alice and felt sad at what she
must have been going through. But we weren't
allowed to contact her and anyway what could you
say to a mother who had lost her son.
Tommy wasn't dead or anything, I knew that much.
But what he did to Sammy was so awful that I knew
that Alice would be really suffering and I had grown
fond of Alice. I really had.
'Where is he?' I asked our social worker a few
weeks after we'd moved in to a more permanent
home. 'Is he locked up?'

130

But she wasn't allowed to tell me anything, and this was too serious to break the rules.

The next *home* was OK and the people were OK too. But somehow I couldn't risk liking them and for the most part I stayed in my room. Sammy was getting better, now, and would often bounce into my room to try to drag me downstairs. But I didn't *want* to be downstairs and I didn't want to get to know them, so I stayed in my room.

When the summer holidays arrived and I didn't even have to go to school I was in my room so much that I got a visit from our social worker.
'You need to get out and do something Mickey,' she said, 'so I've booked you on the holiday scheme.'
'I don't want to go,' I said firmly, 'and I know you can't make me, so  I won't go.'
But in the end I gave in because there were worse things that could happen, like the dreaded counsellor.

The holiday scheme was just for kids in care and to begin with I felt uneasy. But the things we did were such fun that before long I was looking forward to our trips with an enthusiasm I hadn't felt for a long time.
'We're learning to sail tomorrow,' I told Sammy excitedly on one of her bounces into my room. 'I've always wanted to sail, haven't you?'
'Not really,' she replied, 'but I'll try it and see, and next week it's riding!'

'Ah...But riding what?' I teased. 'They haven't actually put *horse riding* on the list have they? It just says RIDING!'
'Don't be mean,' she told me off. 'What else could it be?'
And we laughed for the first time in months.


******


Normally when you were on remand you didn't get to see the prison probation staff, much. But this time it was important that I did because I wanted to get moved to the right prison.
'You'll have to put in an 'app' to them,' advised my personal officer, 'and don't hold your breath, they're very busy.'
'Why are they so busy?' I asked, slightly perplexed. 'The last time I wanted to see them they came pretty quickly.'
'They've been cut,' he sighed, 'about half the team's gone now, and we're next in line.'
'I wouldn't have thought they could reduce *you lot* by many.' I argued. But I was wrong, as I was soon to find out, and the impact on prison life was considerable.


The Probation Officer took two weeks to appear, but the conversation was useful and when she left I felt a bit more cheerful.
'Get yourself into education asap,' she advised. 'Talk to them about your options and let me know what

132

you decide, and I'll make sure that I talk to OCA
when the time comes. You'll have to have a proper
sentence plan anyway if you get a long sentence,
and we can make it part of the plan that you get
moved to a prison where you can access what you
want to do.'
'Thanks, Miss,' I said with a smile. 'Will it be you
doing my sentence plan?'
But she didn't know, and was obviously in a hurry
to leave, so I left it at that.
'Thanks, again,' I said to her as she locked me back
in my cell. 'I'll get to education as soon as I can.'

After she left I sat down on my bunk and looked
around at my 'home.'
'This is as good as it gets for the next few years,
Mickey' I said to myself. 'So you're going to have to
make the most of it.'

The prison was Victorian, but some of the wings
had recently had a refurb.
'It cost millions,' one of the screws told me, 'and
they still didn't close the toilets off, and now they're
cutting staff.'
'Comes out of a different budget, I suppose,' I
stated, 'but there must be rules about how many
officers are on shift, so how can they cut you?'
'By reducing association,' he replied seriously.
'You'll be banged up for longer - there's no other
way.'

I was lucky on A wing as the toilet had a proper
door so you could actually have some privacy. But
other wings, and it would seem the newly

refurbished wings, just had a waist high curtain separating you from your cell mate when you used the toilet. The cells had originally been designed for one prisoner and the toilet had been a bucket which had to be *slopped out*, but that had all stopped now and we had flushing toilets and a hand basin.

On the left wall were the metal bunks with a thin scummy mattress, and on the right was a chest of drawers with a TV on top of it. The TV was a privilege which could be taken away, but I'd never lost mine and I certainly didn't intend to this time. Without it, all you had to listen to was the clanging of doors and the general hubbub of prison life. TV was the escape and it meant that you could dream whilst you were awake.

At the moment I was lucky as I didn't have cell mate, but everyday I expected to get one and who you got was the luck of the draw. In fairness, we were all in the same boat more or less and on the whole you could make it work even if you didn't really get on. But occasionally you got real arsehole and then there was trouble. I'd been pretty lucky for the last couple of years, but it was still stressful when someone new moved in and I had a feeling that my luck was due to run out.

If we didn't have *association* after dinner we were banged up from about 5 pm to 9 am with only each other and the TV as company. And as the space between the bunks and the chest of drawers was only about three feet you spent your whole time on your bunk. If you had a job during the day or were learning a trade or in education you got out for most of the day, only returning for a couple of hours at lunchtime. But if you didn't you were *banged up* nearly all the time. Personally, this had never happened to me as I'd always preferred to be busy, but there were prisoners who seemed to sleep most of the time, the only interruption to their day being lunch and dinner.

Before you were *banged up* for the night you were given a breakfast box which you were meant to keep for the morning. But it was often tempting to eat it during the night so by lunchtime you were starving. I was good with mine as otherwise it was a long time to go without food. But a lot of men found this difficult to do so it was lucky that lunch was so early.

The food wasn't bad on the whole and it was plentiful and filling, but it was hardly 'Jamie Olliver' either and when I got released it was usually some time before I could eat baked beans again!

Of course, there was *canteen* too where you could order things like biscuits and other snacks. But that required money in your account and at the moment I didn't have any. I would build some up eventually when I got a job or went into education, but unlike many of my mates I didn't get any money sent in by family so I always had to start from scratch.

I'd been on remand for about 6 weeks now and the committal hearing at the Magistrates was fast approaching, but it was nothing to get excited about, just a lot of legal stuff really, and as far as I knew my solicitor hadn't dug anything up.

'We don't really have a defence, Mickey,' he'd said when we'd last spoken on the phone. 'I think you should change your plea and get it over with.'

'I'm not going to,' I stated firmly. 'Even though I'll get longer. And at least I'll get some time *out* during the trial.'

'It won't be much of a trial,' he warned, 'we've got no defence witnesses and the prosecution are only calling three. It could be over in a day unless there's some legal argument and I'm not even sure if the Judge will want a report before he sentences you. There's only one outcome, here, Mickey. It's just a question of how long.'

'I know,' I sighed, 'and I'm making plans for my time. But I'm not coughing to something I didn't do.'

******

With Tommy gone my world was a lot quieter, and for a time I hardly went out. Sammy was doing well against all the odds, and gradually we started to build a life with our new carers. They were an older couple this time. More like grandparents than parents, but in a way this was easier as the whole *parent* thing confused me.

They were nice people and I felt relaxed at home once I'd got used to the new routine. But they were boring too and too old to really do much with us, so to a large extent Sammy and I depended on each other for entertainment.

The summer holidays had finished now and I have to admit that we'd had some fun on the *holiday programme.* But in a way it made the return to term time worse and outside of school I was bored.

'Why don't you go out more with your friends?' My
foster mother asked innocently one rainy Saturday.
But my mates had been Tommy's mates so that
wasn't possible.
'I'm fine,' I snapped, not wanting to get into it. 'And
it's getting cold outside so I'd rather stay in.'
'Well I don't think it's good for you,' she said quietly
as she went back into the kitchen, 'perhaps you
could join some sort of club.'
'I'll think about it.' I said to keep the peace. But
clubs weren't my thing so I knew I wouldn't.

As Christmas approached so did my fifteenth
birthday and school was getting very busy. I was
pretty good in most subjects, particularly the
sciences, but I didn't work hard and I knew that I'd
probably left it a bit late to do well.
'It's a shame,' one of my teachers had commented,
'if you applied yourself you could get some really
good grades.'
But I just couldn't be bothered somehow and I was
falling badly behind in my course work.
'I'll probably have to re-sit most of them, anyway,' I
retorted, 'so there's not much point bothering, is
there? I might as well just wait until I fail them and
start again.'
'You've still got time,' she argued. 'Why don't you at
least try to get a couple?'
But she was wasting her breath and I think she
knew it because she stopped hassling me and turned
her attention to somebody else, leaving me standing
there with no one to fight.

Just before the Christmas holidays a new boy
arrived in our class and by the time we broke up we
had become friends.
'I'm Ryan,' he'd announced when we'd first met in
the playground. 'What's going on in this dump?'
'Not a lot,' I smiled, 'but I'll show you around if you
like. I'm Mickey.'

Ryan had been expelled from another school
because he had been caught smoking dope behind
one of the toilet blocks. He'd been out of school for
almost a year after that, roaming the streets and
getting into trouble, but finally he'd been allowed
back into mainstream and our school had agreed to
take him.
'It was only a small fucking spliff,' he told me.
'You'd have thought I was shooting up or something
the fuss they made, fucking wankers.'
'Do you still smoke?' I asked hopefully. 'I haven't
had a spliff for ages.'
'Too fucking right, I do,' he replied, secretly
showing me a small bag of skunk. 'Let's fuck off out
of here shall we? I know a good place we can go.'

## MONTH THREE

It was the day of the committal and although it would only take a short time in Court I had to be there, so there I was..

The van had arrived at 8 am to take me to Court and as I wasn't making a bail application my belongings didn't have to come with me.

I was hungry by the time we arrived and I'd been banged up in the court cells for ages, but the regime was different here and I'd have to wait till later before I got anything to eat.

The court cells were about as stark as they could be and the main thing about this day would have been boredom if I hadn't brought a book to read, but fortunately I had. I didn't read much on the whole, preferring to be entertained without effort by the tele. But there were no TVs here and I'd spent enough time in Court cells to know how the time dragged so I'd made a visit to the prison library. 'Don't often see that,' commented one of the court screws when he came to tell me that my solicitor was on his way down, 'most of em in here can't even read.'

A few minutes later my brief arrived looking slightly hot and bothered and I was taken to an interview room with a small table and two chairs which were fixed to the floor.

'Press the bell when you've finished.' The screw instructed as he locked us both in. And we were left on our own.

'How are you doing, Mickey? You're looking pretty good, actually.'

'It's going to the gym everyday,' I explained. 'Any news?'

'Not really,' he replied with a sigh, 'but there's nothing unexpected either. The case is solely based on your fingerprints being found on the purse and the fact that you haven't got an alibi, nothing else. The victim was staying with her sister for a few days and they both went out for the evening at about 7 and returned at 9. When they returned they discovered that the back door had been forced open and a purse containing about £200 in cash plus some cards, stolen from the kitchen table.'

'I just don't get it,' I said, 'and I've racked my brains about this for weeks. Could we challenge the fingerprint evidence?

'Possibly,' he replied, 'but we'd need to establish contamination of evidence. I've asked the CPS for full disclosure regarding the handling of the purse so perhaps we'll get lucky.'

'OK. Well if that's all we can do then I guess there's not much to discuss. When will I be up? '

'I'll let the usher know that we're ready,' he replied. 'but there's a lot in custody today so we might have quite a wait.'

And with that he pressed the switch and we waited to be let out.

'I'll see you up there,' he said, as he walked down the corridor as I was ushered back into my cell. 'I'll try to get it on as soon as possible.'

Back in my cell there was nothing to do but think or read, but I was too distracted to read, so I just ended up sitting there wondering if there was any chance that the evidence could have been contaminated in some way.

Realistically, I knew it was a million to one chance, but I had been a frequent visitor to that police station in the two weeks before the burglary so who knows.

By eleven thirty I was really bored and hungry, and I was just about to stretch out on the hard bench to give the book another go when my cell door was unlocked.

'You're up next,' announced the screw. "We'll have to cuff you to take you up.'

'I know the drill,' I replied with a nod, holding out my right arm. 'Let's go.'

\*\*\*\*\*\*

Ryan and I were soon hanging out all the time and for a while I was having fun again. He lived with his grandmother as his parents were both addicts, but he seemed pretty happy and certainly had a lot of freedom.

'I want you back by ten at the latest,' my foster mother had cautioned the first time I was late for dinner, 'and if you're not coming back for dinner you need to ring me to let me know.'

'I'll need a mobile then,' I retorted, and to my surprise she nodded and produced a very basic Nokia.

'Thanks.' I accepted it with a smile. 'Is it mine or do I have to give it back to you?'

'It's yours,' she replied, 'but if you lose it you'll have to save up for the next one!'

'I won't.' I stated as I pocketed it. 'Thank you.'

To begin with we just hung out at the park or wandered around the streets, but as time went on we wanted somewhere to go that was at least dry, so we looked for an abandoned building.

'We need to find somewhere that we can get into without breaking in,' Ryan advised, 'and we'll have to be careful when we go in and out. It'll only take a nosy neighbour and we'll have the filth on us.'

For a while it didn't seem like we were going to find anywhere safe and out of the way, but after a few days we came across a boarded up pub and we managed to get in through a back window.

'This is fucking **it**!' Ryan announced as we stared around the empty abandoned bar. 'And by the look of all this dust it's been empty for ages.'

'There are droppings, too.' I remarked. 'Probably rats so I think you're right. These places are probably quite hard to sell.'

'There's shit loads of space here,' Ryan commented thoughtfully, 'we could even store stuff.'

'What sort of stuff?' I asked innocently. But he had moved on to examine the empty optics and he either didn't hear me or chose not to.

142

'I'll have to get back soon as it's Sammy's birthday and we're going out to eat,' I said. 'Let's come back tomorrow and clean this place up a bit.'
'I think I'll stay for a while and explore the upstairs, mate,' Ryan announced. 'This place is wicked!'

On my way home I thought about our new hideout and Ryan talking about storing stuff and I found myself feeling uneasy and worried. He had ignored my question. I was sure of it. And if he was planning something to do with drugs I would have to find a way to opt out. I didn't mind smoking skunk or a bit of solid, but I wouldn't get involved with dealing. The risks were just too great.

******

The committal hearing lasted about fifteen minutes and the case was listed for a plea and case management hearing at the Crown Court in three months time. 'Three months...' I complained to my brief when we had a two second chat before they cuffed me and took me down again. But I'd known it would be a while and it would have been a lot longer if the trial had involved more witnesses so I suppose it wasn't too bad.
'They've instructed the CPS to give us full disclosure on the prints within 2 weeks,' he explained, 'but I really wouldn't get your hopes up. Ring me if you want to change your plea before the next hearing.'

When I got back to my cell I was relieved to find a
lunch box.
'Cheers for that,' I thanked the screw. 'Any idea how
long I'll be here?'
'None at all,' he replied as the door clunked shut,
'depends on the Court.'
'I'll get some sleep then,' I said to the door. And I lay
down on the hard cold bench with my arms behind
my head for a pillow.

What's wrong Sammy? I shouted, sitting bolt
upright and banging my elbow on the wall. But it
was a dream and I was still in The Court cells.
'We're leaving soon,' the screw shouted through the
door. 'Wake up.'

For a moment I really didn't know what was
happening and I was shaking because I'd been
startled awake. But I remembered what I'd been
dreaming about, and I was glad to be awake.
Sammy was much better now, almost normal. But I
still found it really hard when I remembered it
because somehow I felt like I should have prevented
it.

'We're leaving,' said the screw, cuffing me again.
'Let's go.'
'I'm glad it's not far.' I said to the guard as he closed
the door on my van cell. 'It'll be good to get home.'
'Might take a while, mate.' he warned me. 'We've
heard there's an accident on the A27...'

By the time I got back to prison it was dark and raining and I had to wait while all the newbies got their bed rolls and had their pictures taken.

'Hurry up,' I murmured under my breath. 'I want to get back to my fucking cell and I'm hungry.'


\*\*\*\*\*\*


Ryan and I met up after school the next day and we went straight to our hideout.

'I had a bit of a tidy up after you left yesterday,' he told me, 'and I found a couple of mattresses upstairs so I dragged them down and made a sofa.'

'Cool...' I responded, trying to look pleased. 'Was there anything interesting up there?'

'Just empty rooms and toilets,' he replied, 'but the water's still on which is a result, so at least we can have a piss and flush it!'

'Cool...' I said again. Trying to sound enthusiastic. But there was something going on in Ryan's mind. I was sure of it. And I didn't think I was going to like it.

'My brother's coming round later,' he announced casually, 'he's just come home.'

'Where's he been?' I asked innocently. 'I didn't even know you had a brother.'

'Well I *do*,' he retorted rather sharply, 'but he's been away for a long time so I don't mention him much.'

'What did he do?' I asked. Finally understanding. 'It must have been pretty serious if he's been away for years.'

145

'I didn't say *years* did I?' Ryan retorted. And it was just a burglary but he got 28 months for it. Anyway, he's coming round tonight so he can see what's what.'

'What do you mean?' I asked. 'I thought this was just a place to hang out?'

But at that moment there was a low whistle at the back door and Ryan went to answer it.

'alright Dave?' he said as a big lad of about 20 stepped into the room. 'This my mate Mickey. Mickey, this is my bro.'

******

For me, life in prison was familiar and undemanding. But for some, particularly the very young, it was very tough.

As a local prison and Young Offenders Institute the ages of the inmates ranged from 18 to 70+ and often for the teenagers it was their first experience of custody.

For some, who'd had brothers and fathers and uncles go to prison as they were growing up, it almost seemed a natural progression, but sometimes you got a real *baby* who had thought himself *hard* on the outside and was now the smallest fish in a very large pond.

I had been there myself as I did my first long stretch in a similar prison, and where I could I would try to help these hapless lads, but often they didn't know who they could trust, and you could see them just keeping their heads down trying not to be noticed.

Of course you got the lairy ones too. The ones who needed a lesson. But I didn't get involved with that, though there were plenty that did.

When they first arrived they spent the first night on a separate reception wing where they were given a brief induction to prison life and seen by the nurses etc. to see if they had medical needs. But then they got moved to a main wing and for some it was clearly a shock to see all the rows and rows of cells connected to different floors by sets of metal stairs.

As I was likely to get a long sentence this time I decided to put myself forward as a *listener* so that these lads could identify me as someone they could trust.
The listeners were trained by the Samaritans and I'd used their services myself over the years, so I thought I knew what to expect. But the application process and subsequent training turned out to be far more involved than I'd expected and for a while it took over my life.
'The hardest thing to do is to listen without advising,' I'd been told. 'because what you'll want to do is to try to 'fix' whatever it is. But that's not your role and it's important for you to remember that. Your role is to listen and by doing so enable the man in-front of you to work things out for himself.'
And she was right, it was difficult to sit back. But as we practised with each other, all of us with genuine issues of our own, the process became clear, and by the time I had my first real 'client' I was converted.

Time was going by quite quickly now that I was a listener and, resigned as I was to my inevitable conviction I hardly thought about the upcoming trial. But occasionally I'd have a really bad day with my anger, and when that happened I hid myself away.

Hiding was pretty easy to do in prison as you simply said you were ill and stayed in your cell. But you couldn't do it too often or they'd get suspicious and it wasn't a good idea to attract that kind of attention.

'I'm getting a migraine.' I'd normally say as no one could prove that I wasn't. And I'd lie on my bunk all day with the TV down low, listening to the sounds of the wing.

Now though, doing just that, I was still feeling angry and I couldn't stop my whirring thoughts. *How did I get here*? I mean, not just this time, but how in general? Sammy was OK. She was leading a normal life somewhere, and look what she'd been through. Why was I so weak? Why didn't I *stop* it? But I'd been over this a thousand times and I knew that all the reasons were really excuses. The truth was that I'd been a coward when I'd had a chance to stand up for myself and I'd messed up.

******

Dave was trouble and I knew it from the moment he set foot in our hideout, but he was also exciting and within a few hours I was more excited than scared.

148

'It's not that bad inside,' he informed us as we sat on our *sofa* drinking the beers he'd brought with him, 'and once you learn to play the game, it's really pretty cool. Not that I want to go back, don't get me wrong. But it isn't the end of the world, that's all. So if it's part of the risk then the risk's worth it.'

'What risk?' I asked innocently. Thinking that he'd been talking in general terms.

But he shook his head. 'Not now. I'm tired... Ryan, get me another beer, will you? Then I'm going home to bed.'

For a while we sat in silence smoking and drinking, not even a ticking clock disturbing the oppressive atmosphere, but after Dave had gone Ryan and I found an old pack of darts and had a few games.

'What's Dave planning?' I asked cautiously.

'Nothing as far as I know,' he replied evasively, 'and even if he is it's nothing *you* have to get into, so stop worrying.'

'I'm not.' I retorted. 'I'm just curious, that's all.'

'Let's go, then,' said Ryan with a fake yawn. 'I'll see you tomorrow after school.'

'Not if I see you first,' I joked, punching him on the arm. 'I'll come straight here.'

When I left the hideout I wasn't feeling nearly as cheerful as I'd tried to sound. Ryan was my friend and we'd had a lot of fun, but Dave was a different matter and he worried me.

It was pitch black that night, the moon either behind the clouds or not visible, and my footsteps seemed to echo more than usual in the mainly deserted streets. My curfew was eleven, and I hadn't thought

149

it to be that late, but when I got to the main square the clock was striking twelve and I knew I was in trouble. I hurried home as quickly as I could, checking my mobile to see if I'd missed a call, but the battery was dead so there was no way of telling. Shit! I was really in trouble. If I wasn't back before midnight my foster parents were legally obliged to report me missing and I knew that's what they would be doing. It had happened before, just once when I'd fallen asleep in the park after drinking some Vodka, and the whole thing was a fucking pain in the arse.

'Why can't I just be normal?' I'd complained to the Police Officer who'd had to debrief me once I'd got home. But the rules for foster kids were different, and that was that. And now I'd done it again.

'I'm really sorry,' I said as I burst through the front door just in time to see my foster mother replace the phone on its charger. 'I lost track of time.'

'Well it's been reported now,' she replied tiredly as she picked up the phone again to let them know, 'so they'll want to see you again.'

'I'm sorry,' is all I could think of to say again, 'I ran most of the way home once I realised the time.'

'This has to stop, Mickey,' she said tiredly. I can't spend every night worrying. Go to bed now. I'll let you know what the police say in the morning.'

'I promise I won't be late again,' I assured her. And I crept up the stairs to my room, pausing for just a second outside Sammy's to see if I could hear any noise.

'She's asleep,' said my foster father suddenly appearing from the bathroom, 'which is what we'd all be if you hadn't been late. Go to bed.'

150

## MONTH FOUR

The days were all blurring into one as they had a habit of doing on the inside, but the plea and case management hearing was coming up soon, and I was looking forward to a break in the routine.

The listening job was going smoothly too, with a constant queue of the curious and the needy. But overall I was bored.
'It'll be better when the trial's over and you can settle down,' advised my new cell mate who had never served more than a few weeks. But this time, somehow I didn't think so.
'What do you know about it?' I snapped unkindly. And that was the other thing. Apart from when I was listening I was plain bad tempered.

A couple of weeks before the trial date my brief came to visit, bringing with him the cheer of a rainy spring day.
'The fingerprint evidence is watertight,' he sighed. 'Are you sure you won't change your plea? You'd still get some credit, even now, and it could make a big difference to a long term.'
'It's tempting,' I said resignedly, 'but I just can't do it. What would you do?'
'With your record I wouldn't think twice,' he replied earnestly, 'but it's not my decision, is it?'
'I didn't do it!' I said tiredly. 'So they'll have to find me guilty.'
'We have no defence,' he muttered as he got up to leave, 'but I'll do my best.'

'Don't worry, mate. I won't blame you when we lose,' I reassured him, 'and at least you'll get a better fee this way.'
'That'll mostly go to the barrister,' he reminded me, 'and I doubt he'll be very excited!'
'Looks wet out there,' I commented, as visiting time ended and everyone struggled into their coats. 'See you in two weeks...'

By the time I got back to my cell I was wet through. When I left it was dry so I was wearing just a sweatshirt, but on the way back we got held up as there was a fight on A wing and no one was allowed to move.
'Can't we just stand in the corridor, Gov?' I asked pointlessly. But he didn't even dignify my question with a reply.

'You look like a fucking drowned rat, mate,' my cell mate stated the obvious, 'but don't worry. It's almost time for dinner and the TV's good tonight.'
'Thank fuck for that!' I replied as cheerfully as I could. And we settled down for another boring night.

****** 

At first it was just the odd cheap phone and things like toasters and sandwich makers, but before long the upstairs of our hideout was an Aladdin's cave. 'Where are you getting it all?' I marvelled. But Dave wasn't saying and Ryan pretended not to know.

'This is easy,' was all Dave had to say on the
subject, 'too fucking easy.'
'Aren't you worried about being caught?' I asked.
But he shook his head.
'There's two choices, mate, aren't there and now that
I've got a record I've only got one.'
'And who wants to work anyway?' Ryan pitched in.
'When you don't have to. Honestly, Mickey, mate. I
worry about you sometimes. I really do.'
'I'm cool. You know that,' I reassured them. 'What
shall we do now?'
'How about a driving lesson?' Dave said with a wink
at Ryan. 'Seems like a nice night for a drive, don't
you think?
'Sure,' I replied hesitantly. 'I didn't know you had a
car.'
'We don't,' smirked Dave. 'I'll pick you both up in
ten minutes.'
'Better make it Main street on the corner of North
Road,' Ryan suggested. 'We don't want to be seen
anywhere near here, do we?'
'Good thinking, Bro,' Dave grinned. 'I'll be there in
ten.'

After Dave had left I looked at Ryan and wondered
if he was worried. 'What if we get caught?' I asked
sheepishly. But Ryan was laughing.
'He's done it a hundred times,' he reassured me, 'and
we'll go somewhere quiet.'
'Where?' I asked. But he put his finger up to his lips
and zipped them.
'You'll see,' is all he would say, 'come on or we'll be
late.'

That night I had my first driving lesson, and over the next few weeks I got pretty good. Ryan could already drive which didn't surprise me. But what *did* surprise me was that Dave didn't like to.

'You take over, Mickey,' he always said to me as we got out of town, 'you need the practise.'

The hideout was still in use as a storage facility and boxes came and went. But the weather was better now, and more often than not we met somewhere else.

At home, life was progressing very quietly and I was careful not to rock the boat by being late.

'How's school?' I got asked occasionally. But on the whole they left me alone.

'I never see you, Mickey,' Sammy complained one Sunday morning. But she too was busy with her friends and I knew that she didn't need me.

'We're going on holiday soon,' I reminded her, 'so we'll have lots of time together.'

'Oh yes!' she replied, her face shining. 'And we're camping, too!'

'I didn't know that,' I said. Clearly having missed out on yet another *family* conversation. 'But that will be cool, just like when we..'

But I left the sentence unfinished.

'When we went with Mum and Dad,' she finished for me. 'It was a good time Mickey. Don't try to forget it.'

'When did you get so wise?' I asked, happy that my little sister was so grown up. 'The last time we talked you were my kid sister.'

'Well you haven't noticed because you've been out all the time,' she retorted. 'doing whatever it is you boys do...'
'We just hang out,' I said firmly. 'What's for breakfast?'

****** 

About a week before the trial I got a letter.
'At least it's not a bill, mate,' the screw said as he handed it to me with a smile.

It was rare that I got anything in the mail other than from my solicitor, and as I sat on my bunk feeling and smelling it, I was almost overcome.
'Aren't you going to open it, mate?' asked my cell mate curiously. But that is exactly what I wasn't going to do until he'd gone to work.
'I'm getting a migraine,' I replied as I lay back on the bunk. 'Tell the screws I'm staying put today.'
'Sure,' he replied, 'whatever! But you'll lose a day's pay.'
'I know that,' I retorted irritatedly. 'Just fucking tell them will you!'

As soon as he'd left and the door had clunked shut I retrieved the letter from under my pillow and studied it. The handwriting was familiar somehow, but it had been so long since I'd seen it that I couldn't remember.

It's probably just some do gooder. I warned myself.
But somehow I knew that it wasn't and just for once
I was right.

'Dear Mickey,' it started. 'It's taken me ages to track
you down and I must admit that I was hoping to
find you somewhere else, but you are where you
are.
I don't know where to start really, so I'm just going
to come to the point and let you know that I'm
getting married.
You'd like, Tim, Mickey, you really would and he's
got a good job and can take care of us. Oh, and
that's the other bit of news. You're going to become
an uncle!
We met at university last year and as soon as I've
taken my finals we're going to move to Wales where
he's got a job as an engineer. He knows about you. I
told him and he was so nice. And Mickey, he says
you can come to stay when you get out. I told him
you probably wouldn't want to because you've got
your own life. But at least come to visit, Mickey.
That's all I ask.
They wouldn't tell me what you are in for or for
how long, so I can only hope that you're due out
soon so you can come to the wedding.

Write back, Mickey. Please... I miss you...

Sammy xx

156

For a while I just stared at it as if it was the most precious thing in the world. But then I read it again several times to make sure that it was real.

My sister at university! My sister getting married. It was too much to take in. Soon I was crying, though, and as the hot tears rolled down my face I felt a deep anguish. Why now? I asked out loud. Why now when I'm going away for years?

## THE BEGINNING OF THE END

After a few months of driving Dave said I was good enough. 'For what?' I'd asked, innocently. But he left it at that and changed the subject.

'I'm bored,' he announced one sultry summers evening, 'anybody got any ideas?'
'Let's drive to Brighton,' I suggested. 'We could swim in the dark and eat fish n chips.'
'And then we could come back and be bored again,' Dave sneered. 'I need some fucking excitement man, not a holiday by the sea.'
'We live by the sea,' Ryan reminded him, 'but Brighton's cooler, Bro. Why not?
'Because I don't fucking want to and you two can't steal anything without me let alone a fucking car,' he retorted angrily.
'I'm moving the date forward,' Dave said looking at Ryan, 'we're doing it tonight.'
'Doing what?' I asked, looking at them both.
'What've you two been planning?'
'You'll have to tell him, Dave,' Ryan stated, 'because we can't do it without him.'
'Do what?' I asked again, laughing. 'Come on you two what's going on?'
'What are you going to do when you leave school in a week?' Dave asked seriously. 'Get a job?' Go to college? Get a fucking girlfriend and a flat?'
'I don't know,' I replied blandly, 'but I don't have to leave care till I'm eighteen so I guess I'll just mess about.'

'And then what? Dave insisted. 'Come on man it's a big world out there. All you need is money.'

'I'll get a leaving care grant and a flat of my own.' I retorted. But I was beginning to see where this was heading and my pulse started to race.

'You only have to drive, Mickey. Nothing heavy,' he reassured. 'Dave and I will do the rest.'

'But what are we doing?' I asked, both excited and scared. 'You can't expect me to go along if I don't know what it is!'

'You're either in or your not.' Dave stated. 'What's it to be?'

And half convinced that they were joking around, I found myself agreeing.

# THE PLAN

The plan was simple and now that I knew what it was I was committed.

'Are you sure about tonight?' Ryan asked his brother. But Dave was fixated and was drawing a map.

'We don't need a fucking map,' I said. Risking annoying Dave because I was feeling brave. 'We know that place like the back of our hands.'

'It's about timing, you idiot,' he growled, 'and who'll be where, when.'

'Well I'll be sitting in the car, won't I?' I confirmed. 'So all I do is drive when you tell me.'

'And where are we going?' Dave asked. 'Should we just go for a cruise afterwards, you fucking idiot? No. We have, and will stick, to a PLAN.'

'OK. I get it,' I said. 'You're the Boss! Just tell me what I need to do and I'll do it.'

'That's better.' He still sounded angry. 'Now this is how it'll go down.'

'How are you going to make them do what you want?' I asked, suddenly realising that this was not a game. 'They're not going to just give it to you are they?'

'With this!' Ryan announced triumphantly, pulling out a gun from between the two mattresses. 'Wait till they see this!'

'It's a fucking gun,' I said nervously. 'This is way too heavy, guys. You're joking, right?'

'It's not real,' Ryan laughed, 'but it fucking looks like it is doesn't it? And that's all that matters.'

'I don't like it.' I said, watching Dave's face to see his reaction. 'If we get caught it's serious.'

'But we won't get caught,' Dave stated firmly, 'and it's too late to opt out, Mickey. Too late.'

'All I do is drive, *right*?' I was more scared of Dave than of the job. 'I mean I won't actually take anything, just drive.'

'Why do you think I taught you, *Genius*? There's always been a fucking plan and tonight we're going to get rich.'

## THE TRIAL

I wrote back to Sammy the same day not telling her much but letting her know that I was happy for her. 'I really hope I can come to your wedding.' I wrote honestly. 'But it'll depend on how soon it is. I'm innocent this time Sammy, I really am. And I was trying to make a go of it but then *this* happened. I'll write when I know more...'

It's so fucking unfair, I thought as I handed it in for posting. But at least we were now in contact. At least I had *that*.

******

Just before eleven we stole out of the hideout to meet Dave.
'Get in quickly,' he said unnecessarily, 'we need to get there just before they close the doors.'

The night had cooled a little and I could see the faint outline of clouds against the orange glow of the town lights.
'It's perfect.' Dave announced as we swapped seats.
'By the time we get there he'll just be taking in the flowers.'
'What if he closes early?' I asked. 'What then?'
'He won't.' Dave said with certainty. 'I've been watching him for weeks.'

162

'We need to make sure there's no one left in there.'
Ryan added. 'That's why the timing's so critical. But
don't worry, mate. Dave's got it all covered. It'll be a
piece of piss...'
I doubted that somehow, but by now it was too late
and as we approached the target I just concentrated
on breathing.
'There go the flowers.' Dave said as we swung
around the corner. 'Just pull in casually to refuel.'
'I'll have to switch off the engine,' I cautioned, 'but
as soon as I see you running I'll fire her up.'
'Good boy...' Dave nodded approvingly. 'And don't
worry about the cameras you'll be too far away for
them to pick you up.'
'What about you two?' I asked. But I needn't have
worried because they were already putting ski
masks on.
'Fucking hell!' Dave looked really menacing now.
'We're really going to do it!'


******


On the morning of the trial I woke up with a sense
of doom. Until now there had been hope, if only a
glimmer, but I knew that my luck had run out.
'Good luck, mate,' said my cell mate as I left with
my belongings in a clear plastic bag, 'you never
know with a Jury.'
'Thanks, but I'll see you later,' I replied, as I
marched slowly down the wing.

I sat in the car with my hands sweating and my heart pumping like a drum. Dave and Ryan were in the garage and I could see Dave waving the gun, but I couldn't hear a thing only watch and pray, They'd taken a big bag for the money as Dave had said that there would be all the takings from the shop as well as from fuel, but so far I couldn't see any sign of anything in it.

Hurry Up! I urged silently. Before someone comes. But all I could see was Dave and the gun. You're taking too long! I almost shouted. But just then they ran out into the forecourt and I fired up the engine.

'**DRIVE**' Dave shouted. 'Get us fucking out of here. There was no fucking money!'

'It's too late,' I announced as we exited the garage to the sound of sirens and a haze of flashing lights.

'It's too fucking late.'

\*\*\*\*\*\*

When I arrived at Court it was raining and gloomy. 'Don't worry. You'll be back in your nice warm cell soon,' joked the van guard. But I wasn't worried. I was resigned.

'We don't have much of a case, Mickey,' the Barrister cautioned. 'The only thing I can try to run is contamination of evidence.'

'I know,' I sighed, 'and you could tell them that I always go guilty when I *am*.'

'Not sure that will do much good given the stretch your facing,' he replied, 'but if those are your instructions...'

164

'They are,' I said firmly, 'I'm telling the truth.'
'He'll probably proceed straight to sentence,' he added with a fake sigh, 'but it might be worth getting a report if he'll wear it. We'll discuss that later if we're given the chance, but for now just relax.'
'Oh I will,' I said, wondering if he'd ever had a difficult day in his life. 'See you in Court.'

\*\*\*\*\*\*

Considering the charge was armed robbery the 12 month Detention and Training Order that I got was pretty light.
Dave and Ryan got eight and five years respectively, but I was a first time offender and I hadn't been involved in the planning.

When I got out, I mostly stole to fund the habit I'd picked up in prison. But there are no real excuses, just reasons.

Sammy was so hurt that she didn't speak to me for a while, but she came to visit me towards the end of my sentence and promised I'd reform.
'I can't stand seeing you here, Mickey,' she said on one of her social worker accompanied visits. 'I just want you home.'

My intentions were good when I was released on licence, but despite my promise to Sammy the need

for the drug was just too strong, and eventually,
several stretches later, she lost patience.
'Get in touch when you're clean, Mickey,' she'd said
the last time I saw her. 'I can't watch you die.'
'I will.' I had promised as I'd watched her leave the
visits hall. 'I will.'


******


The trial started promptly at ten and after the Jury
had been sworn in the prosecution began it's case.
'The facts of this case are simple, members of the
Jury.' The Prosecutor droned. 'And once you've
heard them there will be no alternative than to
return a verdict of guilty.
On the night in question, the victim, Mrs Evans, had
been called to stay with her sister who was feeling
depressed.
At about 7 pm they both went out to the cinema,
and Mrs Evans left her purse containing her pension
money on the kitchen table as her sister was paying.
At about 10 pm the two elderly ladies returned
home to find the back door open and swinging on
its hinges and the purse gone. They rang the police
at once, touching nothing, and soon afterwards they
arrived.........'

None of this was new to me as I'd read all the
statements so for a while I found myself switching
off. I didn't want to appear disinterested, the Jury
wouldn't like that, but the statements by the police
were both familiar and boring.

166

'And now I'll call my first witness.' I heard her say.
'Call Mrs Evans!'

As she shuffled in I woke up bit. There was
something a bit familiar about her. But it wasn't
until I heard her voice that I suddenly clicked.
'It's the cat woman!' I almost shouted. 'It's the
woman with the cat!'

'Be quiet Mr Spiller or I'll have you removed,'
barked the Judge. But now there was a commotion
from the witness stand and the Jury were sent out.

'What's going on Mrs Evans?' enquired the Judge.
'Do you know this man?'
'Yes, Your Honour. I do,' she replied, 'but what's he
doing in there?'
'He's charged with the theft of your purse.' The
Judge explained. 'Can you tell me how you know
him?'
'Of course I can,' she replied. 'He rescued my cat
and then we had tea.'
'I see,' said the Judge. 'And then he returned and
stole your purse, I suppose.'
'Of course he didn't.' She sounded indignant. 'He
didn't even know where I was and anyway he wasn't
like that.'

By this time I was bursting to tell my barrister what
had happened, my memory flashing back to the
police station where she'd given me her purse to get
out a pound. But the Court was fixated on Mrs
Evans and it seemed like hours before anyone
noticed my frantic waving.

'It would seem that your client would like to discuss this matter with you,' announced the Judge. 'I shall retire for five minutes whilst this is sorted out.'

## THE VERDICT

For a while it had seemed almost dreamlike. But once my finger prints on the purse had been explained and the Crown Prosecutor and my barrister had quickly conferred, the Judge came back in.

'Are you withdrawing the charge?' he asked the prosecutor. 'If so, lets have the Jury back in so we can inform them.'

'Yes. Your Honour,' confirmed the Crown Prosecutor, looking flustered. 'It would appear that there's no case to answer.'

'A nice early lunch then,' smiled the Judge. And the Jury came back in and the case was dismissed.

'You'll be released as soon as the paperwork's completed Mr Spiller,' he said as he stood up. And he swept regally out of the room, his robes flowing behind him like the tail of a kite.

# THE END OF THE BEGINNING

When I came up from the cells clutching my bag of belongings Mrs Evans was waiting for me.

'I'm so sorry,' she said. 'I had no idea it was you or I'd have spoken out at once. Have you anywhere to go?'

I shook my head.

'So you'll come home with me,' she stated firmly, 'and we'll take it from there. Scamp will be pleased to see you, I'm sure, and you can tell me about being in prison.'

'I've been in prison on and off since I was sixteen.' I cautioned her. 'Are you sure you want me to come back with you?'

But the look she gave me was almost scary, and anyway, what harm could it do?

'Well just until I sort myself out then.' I agreed, clutching the precious letter in my pocket. 'I have a sister I can stay with.'

Printed in Great Britain
by Amazon.co.uk, Ltd.,
Marston Gate.